Stark Shadows

by

John Worsley Simpson

A Harry Stark Mystery

Stark Shadows

Cover Art by *Debbie Taylor*

The Wild Rose Press, Inc.
PO Box 708
Adams Basin, NY 14410-0708
Visit us at www.thewildrosepress.com

Publishing History
First Edition, 2022
Trade Paperback ISBN 978-1-5092-4031-9
Digital ISBN 978-1-5092-4032-6

A Harry Stark Mystery
Previously Published 2019, MuseItUp Publishing
Published in the United States of America

He ran with a harness that held a CD player snug against his side. He was listening to Borodin's Symphony No. 2 in B minor. It was in the fourth movement, finale: allegro, and he had the volume cranked higher than he knew he should, at a level he realized put his hearing at risk. But he did it because it blocked out the ambient noise and helped alleviate the strain of the run. Flying over the pavement, he didn't hear the vehicle approaching from the rear.

The bumper was high and caught him at the back of his thighs, just above his knees, striking him with such force it broke both femurs, bending him backward and snapping his spine like a twig against the edge of the hood. His body was tossed, spindling for twenty metres, smashing against the broad trunk of a majestic and ancient oak. The vehicle stopped with a squeal. The driver got out, hurried to where the body lay, crouched over it briefly, retreated to the vehicle and drove away. Later, in a driveway, the driver minutely examined the vehicle for damage, found none, then spent an hour with a high-pressure sprayer washing the scrupulously maintained SUV meticulously, punctiliously picking with a perfectly manicured nail at stubborn flecks and paying particular attention to the substantial bumper and grille. He sprayed the underside as thoroughly as the exposed parts, and was concerned by a shallow dent in the hood where the man's head must have struck.

Chapter One

At six o'clock every morning of his life, in every season, almost since the very day he and his bride had moved into their house on one of the leafy streets running east of Parkside Drive in the west end of the city, Corbett Chesley went jogging through High Park. It was no different that Thursday morning in early September 1999. Coming out of the side door, he was surprised by the sharp drop in temperature since the previous day. It was so cold, he went back into the house and up to the bedroom, tiptoeing to avoid waking Corinne. He retrieved his sweatpants from his armoire and paused a moment to gaze at his wife, her body folded into a tiny bulge under the thick duvet in one corner of their massive cherry wood sleigh bed: her face softly child-like and vulnerable in the thin morning light. He loved her like that. But he loved her as much when her face got firm with determination as she set off to do daily battle in the legal world. Chesley was a stockbroker, and his working day began after his wife's and ended much earlier. But he rose earlier than she, did his run and had breakfast waiting for her when she came down. After work, he would spend an hour at the club, working out, and still have plenty of time to get home and prepare dinner.

As he ran, he was thinking about what he'd make for that night's meal, maybe something Indian. On the way home, he would stop in at Asian Choice on Bloor Street.

Now he was regretting having worn the sweatpants and nylon jacket. "I'll never learn," he thought. He always reacted to the first chilly morning of the season the same way: donning another layer of clothing, forgetting the countless times he had done this only to rediscover that as soon as his body heat rose with the exercise, the extra clothes made him uncomfortably hot. He stripped off the jacket as he ran and tied it around his waist, but he had his heart rate and breathing where he wanted them, so he didn't stop to remove the pants.

He ran with a harness that held a CD player snug against his side. He was listening to Borodin's Symphony No. 2 in B minor. It was in the fourth movement, finale: allegro, and he had the volume cranked higher than he knew he should, at a level he realized put his hearing at risk. But he did it because it blocked out the ambient noise and helped alleviate the strain of the run. Flying over the pavement, he didn't hear the vehicle approaching from the rear.

The bumper was high and caught him at the back of his thighs, just above his knees, striking him with such force it broke both femurs, bending him backward and snapping his spine like a twig against the edge of the hood. His body was tossed, spindling for twenty metres, smashing against the broad trunk of a majestic and ancient oak. The vehicle stopped with a squeal. The driver got out, hurried to where the body lay, crouched over it briefly, retreated to the vehicle and drove away. Later, in a driveway, the driver minutely examined the vehicle for damage, found none, then spent an hour with a high-pressure sprayer washing the scrupulously maintained SUV meticulously, punctiliously picking with a perfectly manicured nail at stubborn flecks and paying particular attention to the substantial bumper and grille. The driver sprayed the underside as thoroughly as the exposed parts, and then ran a hand over the surface of the vehicle and was mildly concerned to discover a shallow dent in the hood where the man's head must have struck.

****

The Identification Unit found little at the scene that Detective Don Tarnow thought was going to be of help in locating the hit-and-run vehicle or its driver, but Tarnow was no expert in these things.

"It must have been a truck, a pick-up or a four-by-four," Frank Furlong, the Ident officer in charge, told Tarnow. Furlong was wearing a heavy windbreaker and a baseball cap with the Toronto Police Service insignia on the front. Tarnow was wearing a pearl grey suit, which went well with his prematurely grey hair. He held the suit jacket's lapels closed and stamped his feet. His carefully sculpted and heavily sprayed coiffure remained unruffled by the gusts of cold wind, but the hair at the fringes, around the neck and ears, was irritatingly fluttering.

"Tire tracks?" Tarnow asked.

"A short strip, just the edge of the tread, on the dirt beside the roadway. Michelins. Nothing special," Furlong said, picking a twig off the arm of his white coveralls and examining it as if it were something strange before he flicked it away.

"Accident?" Tarnow asked. "Didn't see the guy in the dark?"

Furlong shook his head.

"It was less than an hour ago, according to the witness." He jerked his thumb in the direction of a middle-aged woman in a blue nylon jogging suit, standing with her arms gripping her body, the trembling fingers of one hand touching her lips. "It was light already. Besides, he made no effort to stop."

"She heard brakes."

"After—after he hit the guy. Looks to me like he hit him full out, judging by the damage to the body. I'd say—" Furlong paused and took a deep breath. "I'd call in Homicide. He came right over to the edge, but he was in control, no sideways slip. The tread track's fairly clean. He was driving carefully. The road bends sharply just after the peak of the hill. He had to be looking where he was going to follow the curve of the road. I think he came over the brow of the hill slowly, saw the guy, and accelerated right at him. It's as if he moved right over to make sure he hit the guy."

"The woman said—" Tarnow looked at his notebook "—'I heard an engine roar, a big horrid, sickening thump and the brakes screeched.' Now we've got to find out who the dead guy is."

"He didn't have a wallet, of course. Joggers don't usually carry wallets. No room in their outfits."

"Anything else?"

"The guy driving the vehicle was wearing dress shoes."

"You mean like hard, leather shoes, maybe boots?"

"No, not like Doc Marten's. Proper business shoes, expensive ones, I suspect. The prints are crisp and show no sign of wear on the sole or heel."

"Doesn't sound like a typical pick-up driver."

Furlong shrugged.

"Hey, listen, it could be one of those luxury four-by-fours. They all have them now, you know, Mercedes,

BMW. But if it is one of those trendy jobs, there'll be a lot of damage to the front end. Most of those things are like cars laid on a truck frame. Not heavy-duty like a pick-up. Should be a lot of damage. You'd better get the word out to body shops."

Tarnow gave Furlong a look over his half glasses that said, "Don't tell me my business." Tarnow's partner, Ryan Barker, came over.

"Coroner have anything interesting to say?" Tarnow asked.

Barker shrugged. "He says the guy's dead."

"Oh, something else," Furlong said. "The guy's got hair—fur on his jogging pants. I'm pretty sure it's cat hair. I'll be able to tell you later for sure."

****

Corinne Chesley heard the sirens when she stepped out of the shower, but made no connection with them and her husband until she came downstairs and was surprised not to be met by the aroma of toast and freshly brewed coffee that usually greeted her descent. Something made her stomach knot. The memory of the siren echoed at the back of her head when she entered the kitchen and found it empty. She shivered, and when the doorbell rang, felt cold and numb.

Later in the day, she was driven home from the Centre of Forensic Sciences by Homicide Detective Ray Bradley and his partner, Bill Pearce. They had been polite and solicitous. She hadn't wanted to answer their questions. At that moment, it didn't matter a damn to her whether they found the insane person who had killed her husband or not. What difference would it make? All she knew was she would never see Corby again. But she responded as well as she could, although their questions had been absurd. Did her husband have any enemies? Was there anyone who might want to kill him? As if there were another level to their lives, an irregular level, a clandestine level. The suggestion was ridiculous, and she told them so, told them that they had been ordinary people who had lived ordinary lives, that they had been content with their order and organization; their tidy, secure lifestyle; their small pleasures. For the cops to look for anyone who had done this who wasn't a drunk driver or a crazy person would be preposterous. Their questions were so foolish that to the silliest of them all: "Did they own a cat?" she answered only with a grimace and a head shake.

Afterward, she went upstairs and got into bed, pulled the duvet over her head, tucked her legs up in a fetal position and didn't move for hours.

Chapter Two

Exactly four weeks later, Alan Sloane awoke with a pulsing headache. As he tried to rise, a surge of pain pushed his head back on to his pillow. After a moment, he raised himself again, more slowly, on both elbows, and opened his eyes, one at a time, lids fluttering. He became gradually aware there was someone else in the bed, and patchy pictures of the previous evening flashed on the screen of his mind, finally flickering into a more-or-less coherent image. Then, with sudden horror, he realized he had forgotten this person's name. The embarrassment made his head throb.

"God, I've got to stop drinking so much. The booze is destroying my brain."

It would have been bad enough if this had been a total stranger, but that wasn't the case. He leaned over carefully and examined the sleeping face—strong jaw line, a thick, full moustache.

"Carl."

He sighed with relief. How could he go blank like that? He had gone through Cranmer College with Carl, and later, Trinity. Carl Noble. He shook his head, ran a hand over his thinning, closely cropped hair. After a time, he forgave himself and smiled, recalling a joke an art director at the agency had told him the day before, about a retired Indian Army colonel who meets his old batman in town and invites him to spend the night at the estate. In the morning, the batman comes into the colonel's room, opens the drapes, walks around the bed, grabs the colonel's wife by the hair and drags her out of bed, saying: "All right, you, back to the village."

Sloane chuckled silently. He had no batman, but Mrs. Fisico would be there by nine, and if Carl were still there, she'd be scandalized as she always was when encountering one of Sloane's lovers. He chuckled again, remembering the time the cleaning lady's jaw had dropped to find a woman in the kitchen in her underwear. He had relieved Mrs. Fisico's bafflement.

"It's my sister, Nancy." Poor Mrs. Fisico.

Sloane slipped out of bed and stood at the condo's floor-to-ceiling window, staring out at the broad lawn and the bright splashes of intricate flower beds, still in colour with fall mums.

He checked his watch. He'd be pushing it, but he still had time for his morning swim. He slipped on his trunks, pausing to admire his flat stomach in the closet's mirrored doors. He was balding and he couldn't stop the furrows from getting deeper across his tanned face, but the swimming and the squash kept his figure firm and trim. He put on a lime-green terry robe, stepped into a pair of thongs and draped a towel around his shoulders.

The elevator was slow arriving, and he kept glancing at the time—7:30. He was the chief copywriter at the agency, and he didn't have to punch a clock, but he liked to set an example by being punctual, and he had a client meeting at ten o'clock he still had to prepare for.

The dressing room was empty. He hung his robe on a wooden peg and walked toward the pool entrance. At the moment his hand grasped the door handle, he felt a sudden touch at the back of his neck.

****

Grace Spring entered the pool at 7:35. She recognized Alan Sloane by his red-and-green striped bathing suit. It struck her as unusual that he was just floating, because he was always coursing up and down the pool, intent on increasing the number of laps he did in the twenty minutes he allotted himself. Something was wrong. She dived into the pool and pulled Sloane's body to the side. With great effort and more strength than she thought she had, she pulled the upper part of his body out of the water, leaving his legs dangling, immediately giving mouth-to-mouth resuscitation, and praying another swimmer would arrive.

After twenty minutes, she stopped, ran to the emergency phone, called the security guard at the front gate, told him to phone for an ambulance and hurried back to Sloane's body to continue the attempt to revive him. She couldn't have known that her efforts had been futile from the start, that before his body had been slid into the water, Sloane had had the life squeezed out of him by a pair of strong, manicured hands in an expertly administered choke hold.

They called Detective Bernie Bryden, Laurel—but only because his long-time partner in the Homicide Unit was John Hardy. John Hardy was not built like Oliver Hardy, and Bernie Bryden certainly bore no resemblance to Stan Laurel. He was a thick-chested, gangly tree of a man. And neither singly nor as a duo were they the least bit funny, which is why the other cops called them Laurel and Hardy.

Bryden was a mean-spirited, narrow-minded character with a perpetually sour expression, broken only by scowls and sardonic smiles. His wife would have left him years before, had she not been terrified of him. For ten years, she had been having a flaming affair with her hairdresser, Sergio, a relationship with many special benefits: he gave her massages with aromatic oils; he was a skilled and sensitive lover; he knew all the latest neighbourhood gossip; he made her laugh, having a steady source of dirty jokes; and he did her hair for nothing.

Hardy had darting, suspicious eyes and a face like Jack Palance. A notorious cheapskate, he had been divorced for many years and lived alone with a vicious cat that hissed at him. His wife had called him "a miserable, dried-up prick."

While they didn't say so, Laurel and Hardy were a little annoyed that Grace Spring had gone into the water and pulled Alan Sloane out. She had contaminated the crime scene.

"Is this your piece of paper?" Bryden asked Spring. He was poking with a gold Cross pen at a three-by-five-inch oblong of a lined sheet that had been torn from a spiral notebook. He had spotted the paper on the floor, sticking out from the edge of a towel draped over a chaise longue.

"Not mine," the woman said tersely. She had quickly taken the measure of Laurel and Hardy and was not impressed. A fraction over five-foot-two, Grace Spring had a body as firm and taut as braided cable. Fifty-two, she had taught English in Scarborough high schools since she was twenty-three. A black belt in judo, Spring was feared and respected by the toughest students and the most self-serving and obtuse principals alike.

"Bag this, will you," Bryden told an Identification Unit officer, who picked up the paper with a pair of tweezers, and slipped it into a polyethylene sheath, tagged it and made a note of it.

"What is it?" Hardy asked.

"It's a list of booze. Hey—" Bryden called over a uniformed officer.

"Sarge?" The rank of detective on the Toronto Police Service is equivalent to a uniformed sergeant.

"Go ask the maintenance people when they last cleaned the pool, and don't piss around with them. I want to know exactly when the last time they cleaned the thing was, not when they're supposed to have cleaned it. Do you get my meaning?"

"Yeah. I get it." The cop insolently returned Bryden's sour look. The Ident officer handed Laurel back the liquor list in a polyethylene bag.

"Listen," Laurel said, "'Six cases of Mumm's.' That's champagne."

"I know that," Bryden snarled.

"Yeah, but six cases? And listen, 'Four cases of Dry Sack.' What's that?"

"Sherry," Spring put in.

"Thanks." Bryden glowered at Spring. "'Six cases of Johnny Walker Black. Two cases of Glenlivet'. What's that? Irish whisky, isn't it?" He snapped his head around to look at Spring.

"Single-malt Scotch," the Ident officer said. "Maybe our guy's a bartender?"

Bryden turned to Grace Spring.

"So, what do you know about this guy?" He pointed at Sloane's body.

"Very little. I see him here every morning when I come down for a swim. We talk, but not about anything substantial. The weather mostly. The kind of thing you say to people you never really know."

Bryden uttered a sigh of impatience. He made a quick nod to Hardy and began walking slowly around the pool. His huge body moved in stiff jerking steps—like Frankenstein's monster in a business suit.

"So, when you came into the pool this morning, did you see anything or anybody unusual?" Hardy asked.

"Well, I saw Mr. Sloane floating face-down in the water."

"Apart from that?"

"No, nothing."

"There was nobody else here?"

"In the pool? No."

"So, what time did you get here?"

"I told the other officer, just after seven-thirty."

"This Sloane, is he married?"

"No. He lives alone."

"What's the apartment number?"

She shook her head. "I don't know. One of the penthouses."

"Do you always come to the pool at the same time?"

"Do you mean, do I come to the pool at the same time as Mr. Sloane, or at—"

"I mean do you come down to the pool at the same time every day?"

"Give or take a few minutes."

"And Sloane, does he—did he come down about the same time?"

"Often we arrived together."

"So the chances are he was here just a few minutes before you arrived?"

"Probably, yes."

"Which means you must have just missed the

killer."

"Wait a minute," she said, raising a finger. "I did see somebody."

Bryden heard the remark, shouted "Who?" from the other side of the pool, and lurched toward them.

"Well, I didn't connect the man with the pool. When you're thinking about a pool, you're thinking about bathing suits and towels and bare legs and that sort of thing, so when you asked me whether I had seen anybody—"

Bryden put his hands up.

"Mrs. Spring—"

"Ms Spring."

Laurel and Hardy exchanged a quick glance.

"Ms Spring," Bryden said, closing his eyes and nodding. Then, with a patronizing inclination of his head, he asked, "Who did you see?"

Spring gave him a look of disgust, felt like correcting his grammar.

"I saw a man. He was wearing a suit, a dark, sort-of baggy suit, and he had very shiny, black shoes."

"Where did you see him? You mean you saw a guy in here in a business suit?"

She nodded.

"You saw somebody in the pool in a business suit, and you're just telling us about it now?"

Spring scowled at him. "He wasn't in the pool." She drew a line in the air with a forefinger, pointing toward the wall of sliding glass doors, beyond which was a patio filled with garden furniture. "He was walking outside, across the patio."

"What did he look like?"

"I couldn't see his face. The bamboo blinds are

rolled half way down the window. We're on a hill here, facing east, and the morning sun can be blinding, so the security people roll the blinds down half way. I could see only the lower half of the man's body. That's probably why l noticed his shoes were so shiny."

"Jesus," Bryden said.

Hardy shook his head.

"What makes you think this guy outside of the building had anything to do with anything inside the pool? I can't see how you wouldn't have passed this guy, if he'd been in the pool. And how would he get from the other end of the hallway outside the building and around to the other side of the pool?"

"There's a door there," Bryden said impatiently, jerking a thumb at the wall beyond the opposite end of the pool, and Spring nodded.

"Oh," Hardy said.

"Anyway," Spring said, "there is a door by the elevators that opens to the back of the building."

Hardy said, "He could have been a guest. If he'd parked at the visitors' end of the lot, it would have been closer for him than going out the front."

"But, if the person who did this used that door—" Bryden pointed to the door on the opposite wall, "—then the fellow in the suit might have seen him. Let's put a circular together and distribute it to all the apartments."

Hardy shrugged.

"Thanks, Ms Spring. If we have any other questions, we know where to find you."

****

When the security guard accompanying Laurel and Hardy rang the bell at Sloane's suite, the guard was following the rules of the building management. He knew the cleaning lady hadn't arrived yet, so the suite would be empty. He was going to wait the stipulated ten seconds, ring again and wait another ten seconds before he used the pass key, but Bryden gave him an impatient prod on the shoulder. With a shrug, the guard inserted the key. The door opened. Bryden and Hardy instinctively reached inside their jackets and grasped the handles of their Glocks. When they saw a man standing there in a pair of red silk bikini briefs, they withdrew their hands. Their heads turned slowly to face one another with knowing looks, each raising one eyebrow.

"Oh, I'm sorry, sir," the security guard said." I didn't know there was anybody in here. These gentlemen are—"

"Police," Bryden said, sticking his I.D. in Noble's face. "Who are you?"

"Police?" Noble said. "What's going on? Where's Alan?"

"Mind if we come in," Bryden said, pushing the security guard back and lumbering into the suite. Noble backed up a few steps.

Hardy gave the security guard a shove toward the elevators.

"Thanks," he said, stepping into the suite, closing the door behind him and turning to stand beside Bryden. Both of them stared at Noble.

"What is this about?" he said, turning nervously from one to the other, neither of whom said anything for several seconds.

Finally, Bryden said, "I asked you who you were."

"Me, I'm Carl Noble. I—I'm a friend of Alan's. But please, what is this? Has Alan had an accident?"

"Anybody else here?" Hardy asked.

"Just me."

"Did you spend the night here?" Bryden said. Noble shrugged. "Yes, but—"

"Was there anybody else here—besides you and Sloane?"

"No, there wasn't. Please—what is happening?"

"Is that a bathing suit?" Hardy said.

"What? No, it's—it's my underwear. Look, if Alan is hurt or something, why won't you tell me?"

"Did you leave the apartment this morning?" Bryden asked.

"No, I didn't. Please—"

"Alan Sloane is dead."

"What? Oh, my God." Noble put one hand on his stomach and the other over his mouth. His knees buckled. Laurel and Hardy stared at him, expressionless.

"I think I'd better sit down," Noble said, and led them into a living room the size of half a tennis court. He sat at the end of a butter-coloured leather couch, his face in his hands. Laurel and Hardy remained standing. They looked around at the eclectic decor: scattered Chinese screens and vases; African sculptures; a large Navajo blanket on one brick-lined wall; a massive, red-lacquered piece of driftwood on the hopsack-covered wall opposite; the furniture severely modern, leather and denim. Ranged above the gas fireplace were paintings in a variety of styles, from classic pastoral scenes to garish abstracts. One large painting of a sparsely draped, bearded, long-haired nude male sitting in the ruins of a bombed-out building took Laurel and Hardy's attention. They looked at it and then at each other, raising their eyebrows again, never noticing that the dejected figure had puncture wounds in both hands and feet and a gash in his side.

"Your hair looks wet," Bryden said.

"What?" Noble raised his face from his hands.

"I said, your hair looks wet. You been swimming?"

"I had a shower."

Bryden looked at Hardy, who walked out of the room. "Where's he going?" Noble said.

"Bathroom. Do you mind?"

"Look," Noble said, "you still haven't told me what happened to Alan."

Dryden had a twisted smile.

"I was wondering when you were going to ask."

"Jesus." Noble shook his head.

"Somebody killed him."

"What? Oh, my God. What do you mean—killed him? How? What happened?"

"In the pool."

"How do you mean—killed? This is crazy."

"Yep."

Hardy came back into the room. Bryden looked at him. Hardy nodded. He said, "Only one bed's unmade. Did you make yours? Or did Sloane make his?" He smiled humourlessly.

Noble shook his head.

"God. My friend's dead and you—you're making offensive remarks. Jesus."

"Your friend?" Bryden said quickly. "Were you good friends? What kind of friends?"

"I don't think it's really any of your goddamned business."

"Oh, you're wrong there. What did he do for a living—your friend?"

Noble sighed.

17

"We weren't really friends—I mean, we were friends, but—we didn't know each other really well. I knew him years ago, and then we lost contact. I met him again not long ago. You've got to tell me—what do you mean he was killed?"

"I see," Bryden said, ignoring Noble's question. "I asked you what he did for a living."

"He was a copywriter, chief copywriter—at an ad agency, Barnes, Brooker, Adderley. Was it a robbery? It doesn't make sense."

"Yeah, that's what we were thinking. Who'd try to rob somebody who was wearing a bathing suit?"

"Do you know—do you have any idea who did it?"

"We thought maybe you could help us," Hardy said.

"Me? How could I help you? I told you, I don't—I didn't know him that well."

"Are you telling us you weren't lovers?" Bryden said.

"It's none of your business what we were. Why are you doing this?"

Hardy raised his voice: "Because somebody's dead."

Bryden pointed at Noble.

"I told you, it is our business. Were you lovers, or not?"

Noble shook his head.

"God. Yes—no."

Bryden screwed up his face.

"Yes, no? Which?"

"No, we weren't lovers. We slept together last night for the first time. Does that satisfy your twisted—"

"So, who was Sloane's lover? His regular?" Hardy asked. "Whose picture is that in the bedroom?"

"What picture?"

"There's a picture in there of a guy in a skiing outfit. Interesting inscription It says, 'For all the memories.' Could that be a picture of Sloane's lover? You see, you have to put yourself in our position, Mr. Noble. We've got a dead man in a swimming suit, killed at seven-thirty on a Thursday morning in a luxury condo at the corner of York Mills and Yonge Street, in a civilized part of North York. What's the motive? Robbery? Of course not. Rape? I doubt it. Was it a hit, a contract killing? This guy doesn't strike me as somebody with underworld connections, you know what I mean? So, what we're coming down to here is, you know, some kind of—let's call it a personal motive. And jealousy can be a very strong personal motive, Mr. Noble. Do you see what I mean?"

"He was killed in the pool? Did he hit his head?"

"No, he didn't hit his head," Bryden shouted.

Noble started. They glared at each other for a moment. "Do you know who that is in the picture?" Noble said.

"I thought you said you didn't know," Bryden said.

"I didn't know what picture you were talking about. Alan told me it's a picture of his father, for God's sake."

Bryden and Hardy looked at each other.

"Okay, so that's his father," Hardy said. "Look, let's stop pissing around. Was anybody else here last night? Or this morning? Did anybody else arrive and find you two together?"

"No."

The phone rang. Hardy picked it up.

"What? Yeah, send her up. Okay." He hung up the phone. "It's the cleaning lady," he told Bryden. "I told them to send her up."

"I heard."

"Listen," Noble said. "Can I get dressed?"

"Do you have to go to work? What do you do for a living, Mr. Noble?" Bryden asked.

"I'm a freelance artist."

"Any of this stuff yours?" Bryden gestured at the paintings.

"No."

"Well, you'd better get dressed before the cleaning lady gets here. You'll have to hang around for a while."

Noble went into the bedroom. Bryden and Hardy gave each other meaningful looks. They began poking at things, rifling through the magazines on a glass-topped coffee table, crouching down and studying the table top, looking behind cushions and under furniture.

"We'd better have a crew come up here and help us turn this place over," Bryden said. "We've got to find some names, for one thing."

"You think it was a sex thing?" Bryden shrugged.

"You see any sign of blow on the coffee table?"

Bryden leered. "What kind of blow?"

Hardy chuckled. He frowned suddenly.

"Christ, maybe we should be wearing rubber gloves."

The doorbell rang. Hardy went and opened the door. A short, stout woman, about fifty, in a baggy black dress, stood beside the security guard who had brought Laurel and Hardy to the apartment. Hardy beckoned the woman to enter with a jerk of his head and shut the door on the security guard without saying anything.

"What's your name?" Hardy asked.

"Mrs. Fisico." The woman spoke in a nervous

whisper.

"This way," Hardy said. He led her into the living room. "This is Mrs. Fisico," he told Bryden.

"Yeah. You come in every day?"

"Tuesdays and Thursdays."

"I can't hear you. Speak up."

"Tuesdays and Thursdays." Mrs. Fisico spoke the word "Tuesdays" a little louder, but trailed off on "Thursdays."

"Have you been cleaning here for some time?"

"Just Tuesdays and Thursdays."

Bryden shook his head.

"Yeah, but how long have you been coming here?"

"Three years."

"You know Mr. Sloane is dead?"

She nodded.

"Do you have any idea who'd want to kill him?"

Mrs. Fisico looked horrified. She shook her head rapidly.

"Did he have a steady boyfriend?"

The woman looked confused. "I only clean," she said. "I don't know nothing."

Bryden sighed.

"You ever come in here and find him with a man?"

She looked from one to the other, then gave one short nod. Bryden brightened.

"More than once, you found a man here?"

She nodded again.

"Was it the same man, or different men?"

She shrugged.

"Sometimes the same. Sometimes different."

Bryden looked at Hardy.

"What the hell does that mean?"

Mrs. Fisico shrugged.

Hardy said, "I think she means—Is this what you mean? Mostly it was the same man, but sometimes there'd be a different man?"

The woman looked puzzled. She nodded again.

Bryden groaned.

"Look, look, look. You're going to have to explain yourself, Mrs. Fisicallo."

"Fisico," Hardy said. Bryden glared at him.

"I don't know how to." The woman seemed on the verge of tears.

"Well, try. Do your best, okay? Try."

"I try. Two times I see the same man. Two times I see different men."

"That's it?"

"I just clean. Tuesdays and—"

"Yeah, I know, Thursdays. Thanks.. Jesus. John—" Bryden nodded in the direction of the bedroom. Hardy went out and came back with Noble, who was now dressed in beige slacks and a brown polo shirt. "Was this one of the men, Mrs. Fisico?"

She looked at Noble nervously, shook her head.

"No? You're sure?"

She nodded.

"So, that makes four. Four men you've seen here." Bryden looked at Hardy and shrugged. "Okay. Mrs. Fisico, we have to know about Mr. Sloane's next of kin."

The woman's head shook, her eyelids fluttered.

"I just clean," she said plaintively.

"He has a sister," Noble said.

"And a father." Hardy made a motion toward the bedroom.

"He's dead."

"Do you know the sister's name and address?" Bryden said.

"Sorry."

"No mother?" Hardy asked.

"Dead. Car crash. She and his father were both killed," Noble said.

****

Four weeks to the day later, Detective Harry Stark was having a nightmare. It came up suddenly in the middle of what was for him a normal dream—a jumble of unrelated events, scenes that flipped to other scenes without any apparent connection, people who became other people, taxis that became buses that became streetcars. This nightmare featured a streetcar. It was bearing down on him. His foot was somehow caught in the track on Queen Street in front of Holtzman's Deli, and Sid Holtzman was standing on the sidewalk, smoking a big cigar and wearing a red T-shirt that read "Cuba Si" in white letters. He was laughing and pointing. He shouted: "I told you not to wear those running shoes. They don't like it when you're on their tracks. He won't stop. You'd better lie down between the tracks and let him roll over you." The streetcar bell was clanging. The scene faded to black, but the bell kept on. Stark snapped awake, but the ringing continued.

"Jesus Christ." He groped for the phone. "Do you know what time it is?" he shouted into the mouthpiece.

There was a pause before the party at the other end said with synthetic cheerfulness, "Yes, it's eleven-fifteen on a bright sunny morning in November. And, oh, yes, it's a Thursday. Do you want to know what century it is?"

"Ted?"

"Detective Sergeant Henry to you, Stark."

"Not on my day off."

"It was your day off."

Stark groaned.

"What?"

"I want you to go over to the Old York Cricket, Croquet and Curling Club."

"Where and what the hell is that?"

"It's on St. Clair, and it's—what the name says it is."

"What'd you say? Old York?"

"Very good. You remembered something for a second and a half."

"And why the hell am I going there—on my day off?"

"Will you forget about this day-off bullshit?"

Stark sighed.

"There's a very dead gentleman there."

"Is he a friend of mine, or something? Why don't you send somebody else?"

"I doubt that he's a friend of yours. I don't think you know anybody who moves in the circle that belongs to the Old York Cricket, Croquet and Curling Club. They probably have a dress code."

Stark sighed again.

"Got a pen?"

Stark swung his legs over the side of the bed and picked up a notepad and pen from the night table.

"Go ahead."

"Okay. The dead guy is called Nigel Hawley." He spelled the surname and started to spell the first name.

"I know how to spell 'Nigel'," Stark said, shaking his head.

"Do you know how to spell, 'know-it-all jerk'?"

"Okay, get on with it."

"This guy was some kind of computer consultant. Also an avid curler."

"A what?"

"A curler. You know, curling. You slide the big rocks down the ice."

"He was a curler. What's that got to do with—"

"Take it easy. This guy was in the locker room of the Old York—"

"Yeah, Cricket, Croquet and Curling Club."

"Right. He went curling this morning—"

"Each to his own."

"And when he was changing in the locker room, somebody bashed his brains out with one of those big frigging curling stones."

"What?"

"I'm not kidding."

"That's ridiculous. Those things must weigh—"

"Forty-two to forty-four pounds. Yeah, so we're looking for a pretty bloody strong suspect."

"Don't say 'suspect'."

"Don't give me any goddamned grammar lessons."

"Go on."

Henry took a deep breath.

"We've had two other guys killed in the past three months."

"I think we've had more than that, actually."

"Listen, will you. Each of these guys was killed exactly a month apart. This is the third one. On a Thursday."

"So what?"

"All three guys were killed doing a sport of some

kind. The first guy was killed jogging. Hit by a truck or something. The second guy was killed when he went swimming. He was choked to death. Interesting, because the coroner said whoever did that was an expert. Okay, now this guy is killed after he's been curling. You see the pattern?"

"What pattern?"

"Listen. I mean exactly a month apart, all three. Okay? You think that's a coincidence? Now, there's more. All three were exactly the same age. All forty-two. Okay? Now, all three were professionals, reasonably well off. And with the first two, we haven't been able to find any kind of motive. Nothing. They were just your everyday, ordinary, honest, law-abiding citizens with no underworld connections, no drugs, or gambling or money problems, loan sharks, anything. I'm guessing that this guy will pan out the same way. You see what I'm getting at?"

"I guess so," Stark said, shaking his head.

"I think it's some kind of serial killer."

"Ted, this is a new one on me. You find this in the FBI's Crime Classification Manual?"

"All three of these guys were very successful. All three were straight-arrow citizens. Oh, one thing different: the swimmer was gay, but I don't think that's a factor. I think we're looking for somebody about the same age who's a failure. Some guy who didn't make it, and let's say he's built up a hate for people like him who did make it. It could be as weak a connection as that. Or—or it could be that these three are linked somehow. Finding the link may point us to the killer. Now, why Thursday? I don't know. Maybe it has some significance in the killer's life. That's the day he was fired, or something. Anyway, this is my theory. Don't spread it around. It's not for public consumption, you understand?"

"Yeah, you don't want to be made a fool of."

"Yeah, okay. I'm giving you Noel on this."

"Young Harris, detective constable now on the esteemed Toronto Police Service Homicide Unit? That's fine."

"Well, you recommended him."

"I know that. I'm not being ironic. He is a good man."

"Okay, but this is—well, it's not really."

"It's not really what?"

"At first, I was going to say it's a team effort."

"But you realized it isn't a team effort, because—"

"Yeah, because I'm not willing to go out on a limb and say that this is a serial-killing kind of thing, okay?"

****

There hadn't been a croquet mallet wielded in anger at the Old York for seventy-three years, but the traditionalists continued to hold sway, so "croquet" remained in the club's name. Its perpetuation was assisted by the fact that to be eligible for a seat on the board of directors, one had to have been a club member for at least twenty years, by which time it was assumed any radical inclinations for changing things would have mostly vanished,. One would have become so imbued with the ways of the institution that it would be impossible to separate the man—and they were all men—from the traditions.

An unprepossessing, square, unadorned, red brick building, the Old York sat well back from St. Clair Avenue, nestled in a grove of oak and pine. Unidentified except for a small brass plaque beside the front entrance, it presented such an unremarkable appearance that passersby paid little attention to it and many had half an idea that it was an old telephone switching building, or some kind of public-works facility designed to be respectfully unobtrusive in order not to disturb the high tone of the avenue.

Just as there was no reason beyond tradition for leaving the word "croquet" in the club name, there hadn't been for years much more reason for continuing to have "cricket" in it either, although there was still some cricket played at the Old York. The building was flanked by its neighbours in relatively close proximity, but its property opened up at the rear, running behind the neighbouring buildings as a field that included tennis courts, a softball diamond and a cricket pitch. There were enough members who were expatriates of cricket countries, mostly Australians, for Sunday afternoon matches. But the restoration of the cricket pitch had not occurred without a fight. In the end it had come down to the fact that there were more Aussies and South Africans in the membership than Scottish immigrants, who had wanted to turn the entire back field, including the softball diamond, into a soccer pitch.

Old York was really a curling club, although there were many members who used only the gym and weight facilities, the tennis and squash courts and the Olympic-size swimming pool. The pool permitted a measure of noblesse-oblige. The club hired a top-flight swimming coach and permitted young, talented swimming hopefuls—boys and girls alike—to train free of charge if their parents could not afford the exorbitant fees.

Stark drove past the building three times before he

turned into the club's driveway, angry because he knew it was a waste of time driving in to what he knew had to be a power-company substation. When he finally read the plaque beside the front door, he got even angrier, pounding the steering wheel and shouting "pretentious, elitist assholes." He had to sit for some time before he calmed down enough to go inside. He had expected scout cars and Ident Unit vans, and it added to his chagrin to discover that, by request, they had been parked discreetly around the back of the building. Harris was already in place. He was wearing a trench coat over a loose suit with wide lapels, all of which had the decided air of having been acquired at a Salvation Army store. The outfit hung like sagging canvas on his tent-pole frame, and his head was covered with a floppy fedora. He looked like somebody in a Raymond Chandler novel, or rather, a caricature of somebody in a Chandler novel, soft and even harmless, and his boyish good looks made women want to cuddle him. The club's masseuse had been eyeing Harris since his arrival.

"What the hell are you wearing?" Stark snapped. "You look like a goddamned clown."

"Nice to see you, too, Sarge."

"What have we got here?"

"Did DS Henry tell you anything?"

"The victim got his brain bashed in with a frigging curling stone."

"Yeah, weird eh? Go figure."

"Harris, don't use ridiculous expressions like that, all right? Tell me more."

"The building's sealed off. Nobody's left since we got here, but the perpetrator could have been long gone before we arrived."

Stark smiled inside that Harris hadn't said "suspect." That word-usage lesson, at least, had sunk in.

"In fact, the body could have been lying there for a good half an hour before it was discovered. It's behind the end bank of lockers, out of a high traffic area. A towel boy found him."

"What time was he killed?"

"About ten."

"Henry said the guy was forty-two?"

"Right."

"What's a forty-two-year-old doing curling in the middle of a work day?" Stark asked the question automatically. He had no interest in the answer. He was distracted, staring at, but not seeing, a glass-covered bank of shelves lined with trophies on the opposite wall.

"He was self-employed, a computer consultant. I guess he could set his own hours."

"Mmm," Stark said, continuing to stare. Harris followed the line of his gaze, tried to determine what had captured Stark's attention, but nothing was apparent.

"Uh, Sarge?"

"Let's go have a look at this guy."

Harris signalled to a young man behind a counter. He was wearing a white T-shirt with the club's crest on the left side and a pair of carefully pressed grey flannels. He reminded Stark of the phys-ed teachers he'd had in high school. When they had to teach their academic subjects, they would slip a Harris tweed jacket over their T-shirt, and the girls would drool over them through the entire class. Stark wondered what the phys-ed teachers wore today. *Probably earrings*.

"Anybody who comes in here has to be buzzed in?"

"I asked a couple of the members about the security,

and they said it was a joke. There's nobody watching the entrance all the time, there's no video surveillance or anything. The members voted that down. They didn't want anybody to be able to tell, you know, how often they were playing squash when they should have been out selling mutual funds, or Mercedes."

Harris held the door open to let Stark enter, then let the door go.

"You see how long it takes for the door to close? Half a dozen people could stroll in during that time. A year ago, somebody got in here. Jimmied ten lockers and got away with wallets, watches, what-have-you, in the middle of the day. So, the guy who did this could have been from the outside."

"Any sign of theft?"

"No."

They had made their way into the locker room. It was crowded with people in blue jeans and casual shirts, scurrying around, picking at things, like a swarm of ants on a picnic table. The body of a man lay prostrate on the locker room floor, his head in a puddle of blood. Stark recognized one of the Ident officers, Fred Furlong.

"Freddie."

"Harris tell you about the curling stone?"

"Yeah, hard to believe."

"It's got blood and hair on it."

"Prints?"

"It's covered in them. I figure you'd have to hold it in two hands, the way the blow was delivered. What do you think?" Furlong put his hands in front of him, directing his question to the coroner, who was sitting on a bench making notes. The coroner looked up and nodded agreement.

"You'd have to be pretty strong to use this as a weapon?" Stark asked.

"I'd think so," the coroner said. "The rock weighs about fifty pounds."

"Officially it's forty-two to forty-four," Harris said.

"You wouldn't have to be a weightlifter to raise that above your head, but you couldn't be a ninety-pound weakling, either," the coroner said. "You'd just have to be strong enough to get it up there and let it come down of its own accord. The weight of the thing would be enough to crack a skull like an eggshell."

"The killer could have been a woman?" The three of them turned and looked at Stark. He erased what he'd said with a wave of his hand. "Okay. The guy got smashed on the back of the head. He was sitting on the bench?"

"That, or lying down. Unless the killer was about eight feet tall," the coroner said dryly.

"I think that eliminates your outsider theory, Harris."

"Why?" Harris said.

"Well, because a guy—wait a minute, what's a curling stone doing in the locker room? They're not like bowling balls. They stay on the ice."

"It's not one they actually use," Harris said. "It's an old one, not an antique or anything, but apparently a big wheel club member made some brilliant shot with to win a big tournament or something and then dropped dead, so they keep it in here on that table over there as a memorial. There's a little plaque on the table. They touch the rock for good luck when they go out to curl."

"If you had some guy in here rifling the lockers— would he think he had to bash this guy on the head to make his escape? The guy's sitting with his back to him. The culprit just walks out the door if he's getting nervous. I can't see it has anything to do with a robbery. I think this guy did this very deliberately."

"You think whoever did this planned to kill Hawley—with a curling stone?" Harris said incredulously.

"Who was this fellow curling with? Maybe there was a dispute over the game? These games-players can get pretty intense."

"He wasn't playing. He was practising," Harris said.

Stark shook his head. He looked around the room as if he might spot something that merited consideration. Finally, he said, "Well, I don't think we're going to find any answers here. Let's leave this to our brilliant forensic experts, shall we? They can deal with the dead. We'll go have some encounters with the living. Okay, thanks, gentlemen. You can send the body on its way. Harris, let's go see the club manager."

"Grant Sprocket," said the man, who extended his hand from behind a battered wooden desk in a cramped and cluttered office behind the front counter. "I'm sorry, do you mind—" he said apologetically, indicating two steel folding chairs piled high with files and stationery.

There was so little room in the office, it would have been impractical for him to squeeze past them and remove the papers himself. Stark and Harris looked at each other, then picked up the piles of material and faced Sprocket, a short, rectangular man, his long face and skull shaped by right angles, his body similarly described by a narrow horizontal shoulder line from which his torso fell perpendicularly, with no definition of waist or hips. Sprocket nodded and made a short, sharp downward movement with one hand that appeared to mean they should place the papers on the floor. They did so and sat on the unencumbered chairs, the seats of which tilted suddenly downward with their weight, so they had to brace their feet on the floor.

"Good, yes." Sprocket sat down. "Now, you are—?" He picked up a pen, which he poised above a yellow legal pad.

"I'm Detective Constable Noel Harris. This is Detective Harry Stark. He's in charge of the investigation."

Sprocket nodded and wrote down both names. "Good," he said. "How can I help? This is a terrible business. Nothing like this has ever happened—"

"I'm sure this is a highly respectable gentlemen's club," Stark said, nodding patronizingly.

"It certainly is, yes," Sprocket said with a stiff nod.

"Tell us about Mr. Hawley," Stark said. "How long has he been a member?"

"Several years. I'd have to check—"

"No, that's okay. He's been a member for some time."

"Yes."

"Does he come in every day?" Harris said.

Stark looked at Harris sharply. Harris didn't see the look.

"Not every day, no, but quite regularly. He's an avid curler. He's the club's champion rink's skip."

"Yeah," Stark said. "Did he have any enemies?"

"Oh my gosh, I don't think so. He was very well liked, a very classy gentleman. A delightful man, I'd say. He helped us set up the club's computer system and didn't charge a thing, you know?"

34

Stark sighed.

"So you can't think of anyone—there hasn't been anything that's gone on—" Stark pointed a finger at the man. "Now, listen, this is a murder investigation. You can't be concerned about the sensibilities of the members in this, you know."

"We'll be discreet," Harris said. Stark gave him another look.

"These are very important people. But I am being frank when I say that I am not aware of any enmity between Mr. Hawley and any other member of the club. I'm sorry." Sprocket shrugged and shook his head. "I can't help you in that direction."

"Did he have any particular friends at the club?" Harris asked.

This time Stark pivoted on his chair, put an elbow on the chair back and stared at Harris. Harris glanced at Stark and squirmed.

"I can jot down a list if you like, but you won't—"

"We won't be taking them all in for questioning, Mr. Sprocket, no. I'm sorry, were you going to ask something, Harry? I didn't mean to—"

"No, no. You carry on," Stark said, shaking his head.

"I'll do that list for you," Sprocket said, tearing the top sheet from the pad on which he'd written Stark's and Harris's names.

Stark gave Harris another long look, then turned toward Sprocket.

"Was he married?"

"Yes. A lovely woman."

"A real gentlewoman, I suppose?"

"I'm sorry?"

"Never mind." Stark turned to Harris. "Has the wife been told?"

Harris shook his head.

"Would you also put his address down there, Mr. Sprocket?"

"Certainly. I'll have to get it out of the files. Do you want me to get it out of the files now, or should I finish the list first?"

Stark gave him a synthetic smile.

"You know, I think you're going to have to go to the files before you finish the list anyway, Mr. Sprocket. The names are no good to us without addresses and phone numbers."

"Oh, yes, I see. Very well. That will take some time—"

"Yes, okay. And I take it you have the place of employment of all these people?"

"For those who have jobs, yes."

"Oh, you have a lot of unemployed people here?"

Sprocket screwed up his face. "No, there are retired people and people of—independent means."

"Is that right? We meet quite a few of those in our line of work."

Sprocket sighed.

"Good. Now, we'll go chat with the people in the club. Unless Detective Constable Harris has some more questions for you?" He gave Harris an acerbic smile.

"No, no. That's—fine," Harris said, returning the smile with a shrug as if to say, "Gee, sorry to put your nose out of joint, boss."

"Good. Then let's go see these people."

Except for the kid at the counter and Sprocket, Harris had gathered all the club employees and the members who were on the premises in the dining room and posted uniformed officers on the exits. There were seventeen staff and only six club members—two had been playing squash; two had been working out in the equipment room and two had been swimming.

One of the squash players, a man in his fifties or sixties, looked somehow familiar to Stark, but his name didn't ring a bell. Stark asked him whether he lived in the Beaches and got a supercilious look, an indulgent smile and a shake of the head as an answer. He conceded to himself that the fellow had one of those faces, and dismissed the idea that he'd seen him before. None of the members said he knew Hawley. None of the staff, with the exception of the towel boy and the curling rink attendant had seen Hawley that morning. No one had seen any strangers in the club, and no one had seen or heard anything odd or suspicious.

Stark glanced through the written statements the uniformed officers had taken. He looked at each of the police officers, chose the one who looked the brightest and went over to him.

"What's your name?"

"Kobelenski, Sarge."

"Kobelenski, any of these people strike you as—"

Kobelenski shook his head, and shrugged. "I can't imagine any of them—"

"Mmm. Okay, thanks."

Stark looked through the statements again. Everyone had an alibi for the time Hawley had been killed, and yet not quite. All had been with someone else for nearly all the time—except for bathroom breaks and getting a drink of water from the cooler and that sort of thing. Stark thought they made an unlikely lot of potential suspects. None betrayed the slightest nervousness under questioning. Only the towel boy was shaken: he had discovered Hawley's body. One of the waitresses was distraught. She said she had "really liked Mr. Hawley. He was such a nice man." Two of the club members said in determined tones that they were going to have to review security measures.

Finally, Stark told the members they were free to leave and the staff could go on about their business. He said he might have to question them again later, but didn't tell them he doubted it.

He and Harris got the list of the victim's friends from Sprocket, and went to break the news to Hawley's wife.

It was a beautiful day for November, the sun shining, tiny tufts of cloud, warm enough that a coat wasn't necessary. The weather was wonky. It had threatened to snow in October, but now it was almost spring-like.

"Where's your car?" Stark asked Harris.

"I didn't bring one."

"What? Ah Jesus—Mr. Eco-friendly—don't tell me you rode that goddamned bicycle?"

"I got a lift with Frank Furlong. The DS said there was no point in me taking a car—"

"My taking a car."

"What?"

"You have to use a possessive with a gerund."

Harris stared at Stark and shook his head.

"Henry said somebody else would be coming with a car. He didn't say it would be you."

They got into Stark's Chev and headed down the long driveway. "God, this place practically screams with discretion, doesn't it?"

"I think it's antediluvian."

"Oh yes, positively atavistic," Stark said in feigned contempt. "Tell me, why do you say so?"

"No women members, can you imagine at the end of the twentieth century?"

"That's the only thing I like about it," Stark said archly.

Harris glared at Stark.

"Henry didn't tell you about this serial-killer theory, did he?" Stark said.

"His what?"

"That's why he called me in on my day off instead of sending Ricci. Ricci would have blabbed it to everybody. And also, of course, I have a one-hundred-per-cent solution rate. You know that, don't you?"

"You've told me before."

Stark looked quickly at Harris.

"You know, this political correctness crap of yours is all bullshit. As far as I'm concerned, women are good for one thing, and boy, do they ever use that to their advantage."

Harris gave Stark a puzzled, what-brought-this-on look.

"I thought you—"

"You thought I what?"

Harris shook his head. "Nothing. What's this serial-killer thing?"

Stark outlined Henry's theory.

When Stark had finished, Harris said, "What do you think?"

"Anything's possible. Could be some feminist cult, taking out all the classic rapist paradigms although the gay guy wouldn't quite fit the model, would he? At this point, I think the similarities may well be coincidental, and if you examine the crimes from the point of view of differences—for instance, the killing method is distinctly different in each one—you'd come to the conclusion that there is no connection. Anyway, we'll keep an open mind for the time being. It'll be fun to look for a link, and along the way we might just nab ourselves three killers."

****

Patricia Hawley was a petite woman with pale blue eyes. She answered the door of a grey stone house on Duggan Avenue off Oriole Parkway, wearing white sweat pants and a long, blue T-shirt, splotched with grey smudges. Her hands were coated with a white substance.

"Were you baking?" Stark asked.

Pottery," she said. "I have a studio in the back." Her hair was fly-away, but a tasteful and expensive coiffure was still apparent. Erect and appeared tall, Her facial lines and bearing suggested the utter self-confidence of breeding and wealth. It came close to, but didn't reach, arrogance. In similar appearance, a middle-class housewife would have been a frump. Instead, she made Stark and Harris look like slovens. Her open face and bright and constant smile began to diminish and take on a nervous quality as she started to recognize an ominous significance in the presence of policemen in her foyer, underscored by their unease and the sombreness of their expressions.

When they told her the purpose of their visit, the woman's legs sagged and she supported herself with a hand on the hall table. Stark reached out and held her by an elbow. Her eyes glistened and two thin rivulets of tears ran down her now pale cheeks. Stark led her into a room off the hallway, which turned out to be the library. Both Stark and Harris cast quick and envious glances at the floor-to-ceiling rows of shelves, lined with first editions and leather-bound volumes, all behind long, oak-framed glass doors. Stark seated Patricia Hawley on an antique leather armchair. He and Harris remained standing.

"Please," the woman said with a deep sigh, "sit. Don't loom over me. You look like angels of death." She smiled weakly, attempting to be brave, and shook her head. Stark and Harris lifted straight-backed, ornately turned wooden chairs from in front of one wall of the bookshelves and placed them facing Hawley. "Was it a car accident?" she said, raising her head, tilted at a slight angle, her chin jutting. There was a faint trace of anger, a resentment in her voice.

Stark glanced at Harris, and raised his eyebrows. This was always the hardest part.

"I'm afraid he was—" he paused, took a breath, "— murdered."

The woman looked quickly from one to the other with utter disbelief.

"That's ridiculous," she said, shaking her head violently. "Impossible. You must have the wrong— What do you mean, murdered? What are you talking about? Please explain yourself."

"Someone attacked him," Stark said. "In the Old York Club."

"Attacked him?" Her voice was shrill; her eyes gaped. "What are you talking about? Was there a fight? No one would attack anyone in the Old York."

"I'm sorry. He was struck from behind in the locker

41

room."

There was a flash of understanding in her eyes, the recollection of the locker-room theft. With horror, she said, "Oh my God, it was a robbery."

Stark shook his head slowly.

"We don't think it was a robbery."

"It must be a robbery. Someone stole things from the locker room before. It must have been the same person. What else would it be?"

"We think someone deliberately set out to kill your husband. Somebody who had some strong antipathy for your husband, some reason to want to kill him, happened upon him in the locker room with his back turned, and took the opportunity to strike him with a heavy object."

"That's insane."

Stark nodded.

"Yes, that well may be. Now, I have to ask you whether you are aware of anyone who might be described as an enemy of your husband's, perhaps someone who bore him a grudge?"

She gave him a disdainful look.

"Of course not. Everyone liked Nigel. He wouldn't hurt a fly. He was generous and kind. Look, I can't go on with this. I'd like to see my husband, please."

Stark looked at Harris.

"Yes, of course," he said. "I'm afraid we can't take you at the moment. We'll send someone to drive you. It'll be about an hour."

Chapter Three

"Where're we going?"

"Holtzman's"

Harris turned to face the car window, glancing skyward in a look of frustration. He turned quickly to face Stark.

"Shouldn't we be questioning the people on this list? Geez, there must be twenty names here."

"Twenty will become a handful in a sprightly dance of your fingers over a telephone keypad."

Harris sighed. "How's that?"

"Because, while I'm enjoying a well-deserved smoke at Sid's place—and you notice, by the way, I'm not smoking in the car, so you can't sue me for giving you instantaneous cancer with 'passive smoke.' So, while we're at Sid's place, you will be using Holtzman's telephonic communication device to reach out to all the places of employment on that list and find out who was engaged in meaningful labour during the time that our tragic victim—there are two priceless words, eh? Both used egregiously incorrectly in every English-language newspaper in the world every day—"

"Sarge?"

"You don't want an English lesson today?"

"Sarge. Watch the cyclist."

"Who are you? Hyacinth Bucket?"

"You almost hit the guy."

"Asshole shouldn't be riding on a road that's intended for motorized vehicles."

Harris shook his head. "Who the hell is Hyacinth Bouquet?"

"Ah, you spelled it wrong."

"What do you mean, I spelled it wrong?"

"In your head, how did you spell Bucket?"

Harris sighed. "B-o-u-q-u-e-t."

"Wrong." Stark wagged a forefinger.

"Jesus." Harris grimaced and leaned back instinctively as Stark swung around a car backing into a parking spot.

"B-u-c-k-e-t."

"That's bucket. Where are you getting this stuff from?"

"Keeping up Appearances."

"What the hell is that?"

"It's an excellent television program, English, of course, stars Patricia Routledge. You've never seen it?"

"No." Harris paused, meaningfully.

Stark turned to look at him. "Wait a minute. You don't own a TV set, do you? Am I right?"

"Should I feel guilty about that?" he said, shaking his head.

When they arrived at the deli, they found Sid Holtzman leaning over the counter and pointing a finger at a customer.

"You're crazy, you know that?" He noticed Noel and jerked a thumb at the customer. "He's meshuga, this guy."

"Hey, don't get me involved."

Noel held his hands up defensively.

"You know what this guy's saying?"

"Sid, I told you, I don't want anything to do with it."

"He says what the Leafs need is a guy like Punch Imlach. Give me a break."

"That's exactly what they need," said the customer, a cabbie, too young to have anything but a child's memory of the one-time Leafs coach. "Imlach knew how to coach, he knew how to put a team together. He won them the last Stanley Cup they ever won, am I right, or am I right?"

"Imlach was a gate-opener. They all were back then. The times are different. The worst player on the team back then would be practically a superstar today. The coaches didn't need to coach. They opened the gate and said, 'Go to it, boys.' Up and down the wings, up and down the wings. Straight lines, straight lines. No forechecking, carry the puck in, lose it, turn around, get back to your own end. That was the way they told them to pay hockey. Bah. Today, you need strategists, planners, intellectuals as coaches. They gotta be brilliant. They gotta make up for the fact that none of these guys know how to throw a bodycheck. Ah geez, the stickwork—"

"Excuse me," Stark spoke.

"—the Leafs' problems with the best coach—"

"Excuse me." Stark raised his voice.

"Eh? What do you want, oh great defender of peace and justice in our fair community? We're having a discussion here, if you don't mind?" Holtzman said.

"Just make it two coffees please, garçon, for the people whose existence allows you to carry on these mindless arguments without fear of being overrun by the barbarian hordes."

"Yeah, great tradeoff," the deli owner said, folding

his arms. "We're protected from the barbarians by being servile to the Cossacks."

"Pinko," Stark said. "We'll be in the club room."

"Yeah, yeah." Holtzman turned back to the customer, waving his finger again. "Charlie, the only thing can solve the Leafs' problems is they gotta be bought out by a big corporation. These private owners, they ain't got the money to buy the players, and that's what it takes today—money."

Stark and Harris made their way to what Stark had called the club room, a single booth walled off from the rest of the deli, with a sliding door, that displayed a sign that read "Private" when the door was pulled shut. Equipped with a large exhaust fan, it was the cigar-lover Holtzman's answer to the anti-smoking bylaw in effect at that time. Stark flipped the switch that started the fan and lit one of his French cigarettes. The fan's powerful action wasn't enough to protect Harris from the first thick puff of the acrid smoke. He waved his hand at the offensive cloud.

"I still don't understand why you didn't spend more time interviewing those people at the club. It seems to me there's a damned good chance one of them is the killer."

Stark groaned.

"Noel, Noel. Real world. Get in the real world. You have to, you know, in this business. Of course, there's a bloody good chance it was one of them, but what are you going to do? There was no witness. They were all interviewed by the uniforms and by you."

"Let me ask you this," Harris said, leaning across the table, "if this had been a shooting in a Jamaican club in Jane-Finch, or a Tamil hang-out in Scarborough, are you telling me you would just have said, 'Well, thank you very much, ladies and gentlemen, sorry to have disturbed you. You can all go home now'?" He shook his head. "I don't think so. You'd have interrogated them all for hours. *Hours*."

Stark leaned back. He sent a stream of smoke toward the ceiling, smiling as the stream made a sharp left turn, sucked irresistibly into a vortex by the powerful fan.

"Noel, Noel. Please. Black, white, green. What are you going to do? Shut your eyes to reality? This is a different kind of crime. This isn't a dissing, this isn't a gang thing, or a drug thing, or a Tamil thing, or an argument over a girlfriend. What the hell good do you think it would have done to have brow-beaten that crew today?"

"That's not what it's about. It's about the fact that these are all upstanding citizens, upstanding white, Anglo-Saxon citizens, and you didn't want any of them calling the chief and—"

"Noel—" Stark held his hand up. "Please. Grow up. None of those people is going anywhere. If one of them did it, we'll get him."

Harris pulled the phone list out of his jacket pocket, slid open the door and stepped out of the booth.

"I'll send the boy in with your coffee."

The cabbie was going out the door, waving dismissively at Sid, who had followed him to the end of the counter, still shouting and gesticulating, even after the door had swung shut although the subject seemed to have changed to politics. Harris couldn't be sure.

"Schmuck," Sid said, making his way back to where the cabbie had been sitting. He picked up a coffee mug and a plate, stuck them in a bin under the counter and wiped the countertop.

"So what's with—?" He jerked a thumb in the direction of the private booth. "Is he still—?" He fluttered his hand.

Noel was puzzled.

"Still what?"

"You know, is he still being—" Sid shrugged. "An asshole?"

Noel looked even more puzzled.

"What's your point?"

"Say, I haven't seen you in a while. Dickhead said you're working with him, at Homicide."

"Special assignment—for now. Who knows?"

"He likes you, you know, so maybe you can help."

"Help? Help what?"

"Him. Help him come out of it."

"Come out of what?"

"Hey, where's my goddamned coffee?" Stark had slid open the door, and stuck his head out. He blew a stream of smoke out the side of his mouth. It rose at an angle, as if it were straining to escape, but failing. At a certain height, it made a sudden right-angle turn and vanished in a whoosh, consumed by the insatiable appetite of the fan.

"Keep your shirt on," Sid said, waving a hand at Stark.

"That's getting kind of tough. This bloody fan is trying to suck it right off my back. You turn this thing up, or something? God." Stark slid the door shut with a bang.

"You see what I mean?" Sid said.

Noel gave a dry chuckle.

"Not really."

"He's really bitter."

"Sounds the same as he always does to me."

"Have you seen him cry?"

"What?"

"Have you seen him cry?"

"You must be kidding."

"I'm not kidding. I thought you and him were—"

"I haven't seen him since the last case we worked on."

Sid sighed.

"Maybe you can't help."

"What's the problem?"

"Carol left him."

"Carol who?"

"You know. Carol Weems."

Harris pointed a finger of recognition at Sid.

"The detective, the woman he was—whatever you'd call it. The one he was with?"

"Yeah."

"She dumped him?"

"She moved to England. Got a work permit and everything. Set herself up as a private eye."

"Oh, yeah?"

"All because of him."

"Stark?"

"He wouldn't, you know, commit himself."

Noel raised his eyebrows.

"Commit himself to what? Penetanguishene mental hospital?"

"Funny. She wanted to get married, or at least live together or something, but he wouldn't have it, or it could have been the other way around. I'm not sure. You can only get so far inside Harry and then you hit an iron skillet. Finally she gave up. It was the booze, too. But he really loved her. She couldn't stay in the same city with him anymore and not be with him, so she took off. She was in England on that murder case and fell in love with the country." Sid shrugged.

Stark shouted again, this time without opening the door:

"What the hell are you doing out there?"

"Yeah, yeah," Sid answered. He leaned toward Noel. "See what you can do with him, will ya? He's drinkin' an awful lot. It's going to kill him." He called out to Stark, "I'm coming, you miserable bastard."

"Oh, say, listen, Sid, mind if I use your phone? I've got a few calls to make."

"Use this." Sid handed Harris a portable phone. "This is my residence phone. You can take it to one of the booths."

"Residence phone? Must be a pretty powerful portable. What, do you live nearby?"

"I live upstairs, for God's sake. Didn't you know that?"

"No."

"Ever since my divorce."

Sid took a mug of coffee to Stark. Harris went and sat in a booth, spread the list on the table and began making his phone calls. Sid brought him cups of coffee and a chocolate doughnut. Stark slept in the private booth. Customers came and went. Sid was unctuous with some, snippy with others, argued with a few, including two uniformed cops who gave Harris suspicious looks. It took the detective constable an hour and a half to complete the calls. He stood and stretched, walked slowly to the back booth. Sid was smoking a cigar and reading the Racing Form. Stark was awake and reading a book. He looked up at Harris over his half-glasses.

"So? Any luck?"

"What are you reading?"

Stark showed him the title *Wellington's Peninsular War*.

"Christ," Harris said.

"Well?" Stark said.

Harris shrugged. "There are twenty-two names here. I've managed to eliminate ten."

"How?"

"Six were at work. Two were at home with the flu or something. Two are out of the country."

"How do you know all this for sure?"

"Because in each case, someone else was able to verify that they were there. All six at work had secretaries who confirmed that their bosses had been in the office all morning."

"What'd you tell 'em? That you were investigating a murder?"

"No. I said it was a routine police investigation involving an associate of their boss and that I wouldn't have to bother their boss or pursue the matter any further if they could confirm he had been in his office."

"And what about the two at home?"

"I talked to one wife and one housekeeper."

"Okay, so we've got twelve to work on. We might have to speak to the others as well. We'll see what we get out of these. At least we know it's not likely any of the ten was the killer. So, you take six and I'll take six and we'll track them down and have a little chat. We want to know what they know about what's-his-name, the victim."

The forensic people found nothing of any value on the curling stone, but they were able to say—with the extreme caution that had become the hallmark of the Centre of Forensic Sciences since they had been badly burned in a couple of recent notorious cases—that their examination did not reveal anything that excluded the stone as the murder weapon.

There was nothing of significance among Hawley's belongings removed from his trousers and his locker at the club: a wallet with four credit cards, fifteen dollars in cash, a receipt from a florist's for two dozen roses, an appointment card for an optometrist, birth certificate, driver's licence and a photograph of Hawley's wife. There were car keys and house keys and two locker keys stamped OYCCC. There was a comb, a cell phone, a pocket calculator and a digital watch. When they got outside the Centre of Forensic Sciences on Grosvenor Street, Stark turned to Harris and said, "I don't think we're going to find this guy."

Harris gave Stark a look of disbelief. "Why do you say that?"

"Look," Stark said, holding up a finger for each point he made, "we've got no forensic evidence. We've got no witness. The most maybe we can hope for is motive and opportunity." He shuffled his feet, scrunched up his shoulders. "In other circumstances that might be enough to apply sufficient pressure to get a confession, but these people are rich."

Harris gave him a look of disgust. "What difference does that make?"

Stark held a forefinger aloft to emphasize a meaningful pause.

"It means they're bloody arrogant. These people

won't be bullied. They're used to doing the bullying."

Harris sighed. "This isn't like you."

Stark glared at him. "What are you talking about? Don't say crap like that. Don't throw clichés at me, Harris. Don't do it."

Harris held his hands up. He shook his head. "Sorry, sorry. So, what now?"

Harris waited for an answer, and when, after a few seconds he didn't get one, turned to face Stark and saw the man was staring across the street. At a woman. It was a cold day, and the woman was wearing a long coat, a plain, brown coat that concealed her figure. There was nothing striking about her facial features. She was an ordinary-looking, middle-aged woman with an ordinary face and an ordinary manner of walking, and Stark was staring at her as if she were something special.

Finally, he turned. "What did you say?"

Harris looked at him for a moment. "I said, 'What are we going to do now?' "

"Mmm." Stark was still not completely back from wherever he'd been.

"I don't know," he said in an absent, almost vacant way. He tossed a hand in the air, like the gesture of a drunk. "I don't know. Talk to these people on the list."

It took them until the following Tuesday to find and interview everyone, except the two who were still out of the country. In the middle of that, Stark and Harris had attended Hawley's autopsy, which told them nothing they didn't already know, except that the victim was in excellent physical condition and had no apparent health problems.

Later, after they had conducted the interviews and had come up with nothing, Stark said, "You know, I'm beginning to think our killer is a nut. Everybody has made this Hawley out to be the most unremarkable, the nicest, quietest, most-restrained, cleanest-living character in the history of the world. In fact, you know, he's a bit too good to be true. Loved his wife, never played around, didn't drink, didn't gamble. So, if what they say is true, how can you imagine somebody who could be pissed off at him enough to kill him? While he sounds like such a boring jerk, l might have killed him just on principle, but I didn't know him. So, maybe it was a random thing, maybe it was a nut. Maybe some schizo wandered in off the street and saw the face of the devil in the male-pattern bald spot on the back of his head, and smashed it to death with the handiest heavy object."

Harris raised his eyebrows.

Stark seemed to come around and get more businesslike.

"Maybe the wife can shed some light. You'd better go see her again. Take your time with her, get everything you can out of her. Take lots of notes. Pump her, but, you know, pump her slowly, encourage her to think about things, to explore things, to—well, you know. Find out everything you can about the guy: Who were his clients? What was his background? How long had they been married? Where'd he go to school? Who was his closest friend? You know, everything you can."

"You don't want to come along?"

"No—you're more her age. I think she might open up more to you if you're alone. Let me know."

"Can I ask you what you're going to do?"

"No, you can't."

****

Patricia Hawley was dressed exactly as she had been

the first time they'd interviewed her. The same powder-smudged hands and clothes and face. But now she looked tired and drawn. The brightness was absent from the pale blue eyes, and the lines of her face were deeper. Her smile was thinner, but she did smile. She was angry at so many things she would have had trouble listing them. She was especially angry at the police, and told Harris that, although smiling when she said it.

"I'm sorry, but you don't seem to be doing anything," she said.

Harris looked sheepish. "That's the way police work is, I'm afraid. It often looks as if we're doing nothing, but, believe me, we've been working on your husband's case constantly. There's a lot of little details. It all takes time."

She nodded. "It's just that I can't help thinking it's my husband who's dead. He didn't mean anything to you. You didn't know him. You'd never heard of him. Why should you care?"

Harris puffed up. "Oh, I can assure you—"

"I know." She nodded, kept nodding. "I'm sure you're doing your best. Can I get you a coffee? I'm going to have one."

Harris gave a little tilt of the head and a small, boyish smile. "Sure, just black."

They were standing in the foyer, which was lit only by the watery November daylight seeping through leaded glass panels on either side of the arched door.

"This way," she said, and led him into the kitchen, which was immense and old-fashioned in a way Stark would have found contrived, but impressed Harris. He liked the black-and-white ceramic tile and the mottled Formica-topped table with the grooved chrome rim and the slanting, strut-supported chrome legs, and the matching stuffed vinyl-covered chairs. He admired the deep, white, ceramic double sink and the shiny old faucets. He liked the tiny window over the sink and the milled pink curtain that framed it. He was especially taken with the massive, heavy-duty, professional-looking, stainless-steel gas stove. And even the coveted cutting-board-topped island and the wrought-iron ring suspended above it by four thick strands of black chain, the ring sprouting hooks from which dangled heavy aluminum and cast-iron, professional-style pots and pans. He adored the broad moulding that ran along the tops of the nine-foot-high walls, and the plate rail that paralleled the moulding, the rail bearing an eclectic collection of antique decorative items.

She made the coffee in a glass immersion coffee-maker. They sat at the table, which was bare except for the coffee-maker and two wide-mouthed mugs, green with an Aztec-looking pattern, like cafe-au-lait bowls, but with handles.

"Tell me about your husband."

"What about him?"

"Well, just—where was he from? A little bit of his history."

"He was born in Collingwood. His father owned a car dealership."

"Owned? Is his father dead?"

"Yes."

"Mother?"

"They were divorced when Nigel was a young child. She went to live in France, remarried. Nigel never knew her. I have no idea how to get in touch with her. No one does. I've tried."

"Nigel was a computer consultant?"

"Yes. He worked out of the house. His office is upstairs."

"What about—I'm sorry to get personal—what about money? Any financial problems? Working on your own can be dicey."

"Nigel's father had already sold the car dealership when he died. I handled all the finances. Believe me, we had no difficulties in that area. Nigel was very well paid for what he did."

"I don't want to seem to be prying into sensitive matters, but I have to ask these questions. Did he have any personal problems, drink, drugs? Anything like that?"

She laughed.

"Nigel didn't even smoke. He was very conscious of his health." She sighed. "He was a very serious person."

"You've had time to think. Is there anyone who might have had a grudge against your husband?" Harris held his hands up. "Again, I'm sorry, but is it possible that—that there might have been anything sexual?"

"Nigel? No. No chance. Even without knowing that that wasn't in his nature, l can tell you that he would have had absolutely no opportunity for anything like that. He was with me almost all the time. The only time he was on his own was when he went to visit a client, and that was very rare. They contacted him by phone and email. We went to the gym together. The only other occasion on which he went anywhere regularly on his own was when he went to curl." The realization that that part of his life had been the scene of the end of his life stopped her. Her shoulders drooped. She shook it off and went on. "And there were so many times that I had to call him at the Old York to relay a message from a client that I know he couldn't have been using that as a cover for any dalliance. That's out of the question."

Harris gave her a sympathetic smile."You have no children?"

"No." She sighed. "We were talking about starting a family."

There was a significant silence. Harris cleared his throat. His questions were producing only pain. He was going to have nothing to report to Stark. Finally he said, "So, have you known each other long? Where did you meet?"

That, at least, made her smile weakly.

"It was at a dance. I was at Havergal; Nigel was at Cranmer College. They used to hold joint dances. Nigel was very shy. I asked him to dance. He didn't know what to say to a girl. I liked him immediately, maybe because he wasn't smooth like a lot of the others. He wasn't full of himself. After we danced, I asked him whether he'd like some punch. He just nodded. I kept asking him questions. He answered yes or no. Finally, I said something about computers, and that lit him up. He was one of the first to be into computers. I didn't understand a thing he was talking about, but I pretended to be interested.

"Anyway, two weeks went by, and I'd almost forgotten about him, when he phoned. Actually he called three times, hung up the first two, and finally spoke the third time. It took me a while to figure out who was calling. He asked me whether I'd like to go to a lecture on the future of artificial intelligence, and I said yes. We went on a few dates after that, but it was the last year of high school, and he went off to Carleton and I went to

Western, and we lost contact until we were both in our senior years, and he came to Western for some computer conference and we ran into each other on the campus. One thing led to another, and we were engaged six months later and married two years after that. We lived in Ottawa. He got a job with the Ministry of Industry, Trade and Commerce. We were there for quite a few years before we moved back to Toronto and he set up on his own."

****

"Any chance Hawley was gay?"

Stark and Harris were sitting in an interview room in the Homicide Unit with Ted Henry.

"I don't think so," Stark answered Henry. "I have no reason to think he was. Why?"

"The second guy, Alan Sloane, was gay," Henry said.

"So?"

"So, we're looking for a connection, are we not?"

"Well, you've just heard my description. I told you she said, don't go into any sexual thing because it wouldn't lead anywhere."

"Yeah, but maybe that's because she doesn't want us to find out something about him that might be embarrassing," Henry said. "I mean, why did she specifically say to stay away from anything sexual?"

"Because I think she wants us to find the killer, and that route would be a waste of time," Harris said, with a slight edge to his voice.

"Maybe."

"I think we should look into it," Stark said.

"God."

"I agree with Harry. What's your problem?" Henry

said.

"I don't think he was gay."

"You don't know anything about the guy," Stark said. "What you got from the wife is useless. So far we've got no reason for the guy's being killed. Nothing."

"Well, what did you find out about Sloane?"

"Well, Sloane was strangled, and a curling stone was the weapon in the Hawley killing. And the first guy, Chesley, was hit by an SUV. There's nothing, no common thread that would help us identify a killer. Well, that's it, then," Stark said, raising his hands, palms up.

"What?" Henry leaned toward Stark.

"It has to be a woman."

"Why?"

Harris shook his head.

"He's making some kind of sexist joke, Sarge."

"For God's sake, Harry, will you cut it out."

"Okay, listen. If it's a serial killer, there must be some other piece of forensic that ties these three together. Something."

"Well, one thing. At the scene of the truck killing, they found a footprint, like the print of a dress shoe. They matched a piece of marking from the heel, and the shoes are Dacks, expensive shoes."

"You're not going to tell us they found the same print—"

"No, but at the pool death, there was a witness who saw somebody wearing a suit. It could be the guy dresses like a businessman."

"What about at the curling club?" Harris said. "Maybe we should ask if anybody saw somebody in a suit."

"Jesus, Noel, it's a businessman's club. Half the

people in there would come in wearing suits."

"It's something, I guess," Stark said. "We look for a well-dressed killer."

Henry and Harris ignored the comment.

Harris said, "I think we have to try to find somebody the victims knew in common."

"I still want to check out the gay thing," Stark said.

Henry said, "I think Harry's right. The only one that has anything off-centre is the gay guy."

"Off-centre?" Harris said, shaking his head.

"Maybe the other two were in the closet," Henry said. "We should at least eliminate it."

"Noel, I want you to look into that."

Harris didn't respond.

"Noel?"

"All right," Harris snapped.

"And listen—" Henry pointed at Harris and then at Stark. "You know there are three teams of detectives on these cases. Stark, you don't get along with Hardy and Bryden at the best of times. Make sure you keep them in the loop and tell them what you're doing if you have to get into the Sloane death. You don't have to worry as much with Bradley and Pearce on the Chesley case. Those guys are pretty easy going."

Chapter Four

That night in Carbo's, Stark had three Scotches in the first half hour at the piano bar. Morty Greenwood exchanged glances with Ulysses, the owner. Ulysses came over and put an arm around Stark's shoulders.

"Everything all right, Harry?"

"What?"

"Is everything okay? You're feeling all right?"

Stark slowly turned his head to look at Ulysses.

"Yes, I'm feeling all right. Are you feeling all right?"

"You seem a little distracted."

"Maybe it's the music."

Morty looked up from his keyboard.

"The music? You love Morty's music," Ulysses said.

"Sure, when he plays the good stuff, but not this Lester Lanin crap."

"He plays your kind of music later, Harry. Early in the evening, when people are dining, they like more mellow music."

"Mellow? It's saccharine."

Ulysses patted Stark on the shoulder.

"You take it easy, Harry. Any time you want to talk, I'm here, all right?"

"Mmm."

After Ulysses had returned to his usual spot at the

end of the main bar, Morty tried to breach the wall.

"You know Lester Lanin has a great band."

"Jesus. He's not still alive?" *

"Sure. He's in his eighties. He's got a company with twenty orchestras, sixteen hundred musicians. He's in the Guinness book of records for having had more engagements than any band in history."

"How the hell do you know that, for God's sake?"

"You made the same crack the other day, so l looked him up on the Web."

"God, you and that bloody Internet." Stark shook his head. "Why don't you try reading a book?"

"Harry, don't use up all your malevolence so quickly. You've got a whole night of unpleasantness ahead of you."

"Bugger off"

"Oh, very nice."

Stark continued to drink, staring at the fake grand-piano lid, ignoring Morty. After a time, a woman arrived and sat two stools away from Stark. He glanced at her, and she gave the flicker of a polite smile, which he returned automatically. Eventually, she asked Morty whether he knew "Ballad of the Sad Young Men," and Stark's head snapped toward her.

"It's appropriate," Morty said. "Yes, l know it, but I'm afraid I have to take a break. I'll happily play it for you when I return."

Morty paused behind Stark on his way past him. "Are you coming?" he said. Stark usually went with Morty for a smoke break in the alley at the rear of the Queen Street club in the city's Beaches district.

"No. I'm just going to sit here."

Morty left with a shrug.

"So, you seem to know good music," Stark said to the woman, who was about forty-five, exceedingly thin, a little worn at the edges with frowzy hair, neck length in an indistinct style. Her face was plain and uninteresting. She smoked long, thin cigarettes. Ulysses had designated the piano bar as an unofficial smoking area, because most of the people it attracted seemed to be smokers. He wouldn't allow Stark to smoke his strong-smelling Gauloises, however, and Morty, as an employee, was not permitted to smoke.

The woman and Stark talked about jazz, and when Morty returned, he played the number she had requested before returning to what Stark had characterized as his "Lester Lanin" repertoire. The woman allowed Stark to buy her a drink. He got it—a Scotch like his and one for himself from the main bar. When he came back, he took the stool next to hers. When the early-evening diners had been replaced by drinkers and the noise level had consequently increased, Morty began playing the music that Stark and the woman liked.

"You get out to clubs a lot?" Stark asked her.

She nodded. "Most nights."

"Is that so?"

The woman matched Stark Scotch for Scotch, and he was pleased that she paid for as many as he did. Eventually, they staggered out of Carbo's together. It was raining heavily, big drops splashing up from the pavement, glistening in the streetlights. Stark pulled his raincoat up over his head and draped it over the head of the woman. They swayed down the street to Stark's apartment on Queen, above Jimmy Yu's dental clinic. They engaged in an awkward and frenetic sort of lovemaking and fell asleep, Stark still wearing his shirt and socks, while she was still in her sweater. When Stark awoke in the morning, she had gone.

Stark rolled over in bed, pushing Powder, his cat, on to the floor. The cat had been occupying the warm spot the woman had left. Startled by Stark's sudden movement, she scurried back into her closet and into her little nest behind a pile of underwear. Since Weems didn't come by anymore, there was again much scattered clothing for the cat to sleep on.

Chapter Five

Sid Holtzman shook his head as Stark came through the door of the coffee shop. Sid gave Noel Harris a what-did-I-tell-you look.

"Coffee, quick," Stark moaned. It was still raining, and the effects of it intensified the down-and-out look the detective presented, his curly hair sodden, drooping on his forehead.

"Christ, you look like a piece of turd somebody just scraped off his boot. What the hell's the matter with you, Stark? Jesus." Holtzman plunked down a mug of coffee so roughly it slopped on to the counter.

"Rough night?" Harris asked, unsmiling.

"Don't start."

"Okay. I'm not trying to start anything. Just making polite noises."

"Yeah, well, don't make any noises."

Stark's hand shook slightly as he lifted the coffee to his lips. He put the mug down gingerly, took a deep breath, got down from the stool, removed his raincoat, shook it and draped it over the back of a booth.

Sid opened his mouth to protest, and then shook his head and waved both hands dismissively.

Stark cleared his throat noisily and gave Harris a little nod.

"So, what did you find out?"

Harris sighed.

"He wasn't gay. I went to a couple of places I know, showed his picture discreetly to some people who tend to know what's going on. They'd never seen him before. And then I interviewed the chap who had been in Sloane's apartment the morning he was killed."

"By the way, Henry doesn't know you're gay, does he?"

"Not as far as I know."

"Keep it that way. So, what did the guy who spent the night with Sloane have to say?"

"He didn't know Hawley either. Mind you, he didn't know Sloane all that well."

"Well enough."

"God. You know, with all due respect to your rank, I've got to say you're being a real prick this morning."

"What else?"

"Well, I went to the curling club again. I spoke to people at random, asked them whether there was anything unusual about Hawley." Harris rolled his eyes. "Anyway, they said he was—I don't know—dull, really, I guess. Just absolutely ordinary, quiet, very conservative. Good curler. Nothing. And I asked whether anybody knew what gym he went to, and somebody did, so I went there. The manager had never heard of him."

"What?"

"Well, wait. I showed him the picture, and he said, 'Oh, yeah, I know him, but only because of his wife. She's a knock-out,' he said. 'They always come in together.' 'Did he ever come in alone?' I asked. The guy said never, always with his wife. So, what does that look like?"

"It looks like it's too late to say the guy should get a life."

Harris shook his head.

"Anyway, I don't think you have to worry about stepping on Laurel and Hardy's toes."

"Why not?"

"Because they've all but written it off as a gay lovers' quarrel. In their report to Henry, they say their only suspect is Carl Noble, the chap who was in Alan Sloane's apartment. The bastards have all but taken him down to Commissioners Street and given him a tune-up. They interviewed him three times downtown. Gave him a hell of a rough time. Pair of real homophobes, those two. Bastards."

"Even so, we don't want them to know we're working on their case. Bradley and Pearce have just about closed the book on the Chesley killing, too."

"They have?"

"Yeah. They're convinced that it was a simple hit-and-run. The reason being that there is simply no motive. The Chesley guy was just as perfect a citizen as the other two."

"Well, maybe they're right. Maybe those other two swine are right, too. I still think Ted's reaching to try to make a connection between the three."

"Among the three."

Harris sighed.

"Okay, look, we've got to eliminate things. I think we've got to find either that there is a link among the three, or there isn't," Stark said.

"How do we do that?"

"Go right back to their birth, see whether they crossed paths anywhere in their lives."

"That's a tall order."

"Maybe, maybe not. We won't know until we do it."

As it turned out, the connection among the three victims was discovered so quickly and was so obvious that the two detectives missed a second, equally significant parallel.

"All three," Stark said, smiling. "They all went to Cranmer College, that great bastion of reaction."

"And Orange Protestantism. You're a Catholic, aren't you?"

"I'm a nothing," Stark said. "Actually, I'm keeping my options open. Not taking any chances."

Harris chuckled.

"Listen, not only did they attend the same school, they went there at the same time, exactly the same years. They knew each other," Stark said.

Chapter Six

When Cranmer College was built, early in the nineteenth century, it was surrounded by farmland. Its stone and brick buildings now stand close to the geographical centre of the city, buffered by wide lawns, sheltered by massive oaks behind an iron railing through which only the residences of the rich and powerful can be seen, and from which the school draws many of its boys.

Driving through its towering gates, Stark felt immediately out of place. He had telephoned to say he was coming and had been slightly intimidated by the precise, clipped diction of the secretary he had spoken to, who had demanded to know the purpose of his request to visit the institution. She had become particularly unpleasant and noticeably uneasy when told he was seeking information on former students. The associate principal to whom he had been connected made him feel more comfortable. He was surprised to hear a woman's voice. She introduced herself as Diane Shapton. She was friendly and gracious, and told him she would be most pleased to co-operate in his inquiries.

A delicate-looking boy of about twelve, in a white shirt and tie, and grey flannels, had been designated to meet Stark at the main entrance and conduct him to the associate principal's office. He ran out to the detective's car as it pulled up. He was carrying an umbrella, but didn't open it as he stood in the rain beside the driver's window. Stark lowered the window a few inches.

"Mr. Stark," the boy said with a self-assured smile. "Would you mind parking in the visitors' area, sir. I'll show you where it is." The boy nodded in a gesture that didn't admit of the possibility that Stark might refuse the request, and Stark did as he had been bidden. On the way back from the car, the boy held the umbrella over Stark, leaving himself exposed to the steady falling drizzle of rain.

"It's a bit chilly today, sir, don't you think? Compared with what it has been, I mean. The fall has been quite cool—on average, that is, but this month has been so warm until now."

Stark nodded in a quick jerk.

"Yeah," he said meaninglessly. The kid was making him feel inadequate. At the boy's age, Stark would have been scared to death of an adult, especially a policeman, and would have mumbled nervously with his head down and shuffled his feet. But then he lacked what they call the boy's "breeding."

The entrance hall was predictable and as imposing as the rest of the property, with walnut-panelled walls and a high, vaulted ceiling. Portraits of former headmasters glared disapprovingly at Stark, all in their academic robes, some of the faces bristling with side-whiskers.

Diane Shapton's office was a utilitarian affair that might well have looked the same when the building was erected, except for the computer screen at one end of a massive oak desk, which stood in front of two tall and narrow leaded windows. The walls were a watery green and in need of paint. The flooring was in black-and-white tiles. The decor could have charitably been called spartan. An anaemic spider plant drooping from a small glass vase atop a tall, standard-green filing cabinet was the only non-functional item in sight. Two certificates in black frames attested to Diane Shapton's having attained a baccalaureate in English from the University of Western Ontario and a master's degree in the same subject from the University of Toronto. Apart from a bulletin board, on which five or six items were neatly pinned in even rows, there was nothing else on the walls. There was a crack in the plaster in one corner. Stark smiled inwardly at the notion that the management didn't want visiting parents to get the impression that any part of the extortionate fees they paid to have their offspring educated was being wasted on frills for the staff.

Shapton was an attractive woman, wearing a navy, well-tailored suit that enhanced a trim, but well-rounded figure, Stark noted approvingly. Her jet-black hair was pulled into a roll at the back of her head. Stark was having trouble with her age. She had a youthful, pretty face, tastefully made up, but there was a hint of tiny crow's feet at the corners of her eyes. He quickly worked out the Roman numerals on the BA—not without her noticing with a smile. She had graduated in 1967. He figured, with moderate surprise, that that meant she was probably in her early fifties. She extended a hand and gave him a generous and disarming smile.

"Mr. Stark? Or should I call you Detective Stark?"

Stark was tempted to say, "Call me Harry," but he said, "Mr.'s fine." He noticed she wasn't wearing a wedding ring.

"So, please, sit down." She indicated one of two venerable red leather armchairs.

Stark noticed a pack of unfiltered Camels on the corner of her desk. Another surprise. It flashed through his mind that a woman who smoked cigarettes like those wouldn't have much objection to his Gauloises.

"That's a bit naughty, isn't it?" he said, indicating the cigarettes.

"Sorry? Oh, that's embarrassing." She opened a drawer and scooped the package into it. "It's a good thing you aren't a student, or worse, the principal. Fortunately, the old windows in this building can be opened," she said in a conspiratorial whisper. "When the pressure builds up around here, and it can, believe me, I sometimes sneak a quick smoke and blow it out the window. Anyway, what can I do for you?"

"Well, it's about three of your former students."

"When did they graduate? I'll get their files."

"It was—just a second—" He pulled out his notebook. "1976."

"And their names?"

He consulted the notebook again.

"Corbett Chesley, Alan Sloane, and Nigel Hawley."

Stark glanced at Shapton after he read the names. He thought he might have seen a little jerk of the woman's neck as he pronounced them. He quickly returned his gaze to his notes and when he looked up again, the woman was smiling. Stark was impressed with her smile. It seemed warm and honest, a soft, uncontrived smile. It made *him* smile. For a few seconds he stared at her, and then, realizing that he had been staring, looked down at his notebook again. Shapton picked up the phone and asked a secretary to bring in the files of the three former students.

"Well," she said. "The files will be here in a

moment. I'm afraid I'm not sure how much I can tell you about them. That is to say, there is a certain amount of confidentiality we must maintain. If I'm not able to give you what you want, you may have to get a court order. I don't want to be difficult, but there is a certain protocol, and it might be necessary to satisfy the board of governors that all the legal niceties were effected, you understand?"

"Well, sure."

"Can you tell me what—is it some criminal matter?"

"Yeah, but they're not suspects. It would be better for them if they were. I'm afraid the three of them are dead. They're all murder victims."

Shapton slumped in her chair. The pen she had picked up to write the names fell from her hand. Her eyes gaped and her face went white.

"I'm sorry," Stark said awkwardly. "I shouldn't have told you like that. Can I get you something? A glass of water?"

She gave a half laugh.

"Where would you find the water? This is my office."

"Yeah, of course, I—"

"It's okay. It was just such a shock. My God. Where was this? I don't remember reading anything about it. Although, I don't follow the police news that closely. I don't think anyone here on the staff could have noticed or they would have said something."

"There were three separate killings. But we have reason to believe there might be a connection. Please, you must keep that part confidential. I'm telling you because it might help you to help us if you know what we're looking for."

She nodded. "Yes, of course."

"Have you been here at the school long?"

"All my career. If you're asking whether I was here when they were students, the answer is yes, I would have been."

"Do you remember them at all?"

"Well, there are so many students, you know, and—I remember many, of course, but these names don't ring a bell. I'm better with faces. Their files will have their photographs, and I might remember something when I see them."

There was a light rap on the door.

"Come in, Kristin."

The secretary, a tiny woman past sixty, hurried into the room and handed the files to Shapton. She left more slowly, giving Stark a curious once-over.

Shapton opened the files, and studied the students' photos. She leafed through the records. After a moment, she said: "I'm sorry, oh, my pen." She reached down to pick up the pen that had fallen to the floor. When she straightened up, her eyes and her head were moving slightly from side to side, as if she were playing back a scene in her mind. She held the pen up, signalling a thought, flipped the files until she found the one she wanted, and pulled out Alan Sloane's photo, turning it toward Stark.

"That's Alan Sloane," Stark said. "Am I right?"

"It is, yes."

"You remember something about Sloane?"

"Yes, I do. Just a minute. This little code number on the inside of the file folder. You see?"

"What does that mean?"

"It means there's a confidential file in connection

with this student."

"A confidential file?"

"Yes. Something that, you know, could be embarrassing."

"Embarrassing?"

"Yes, well supposing one of our students—perish the thought—" She raised her eyebrows and smiled. "—got one of the Havergal girls in a family way and it came to our attention. We would want to know about it, because it might affect the lad's behaviour and his marks, perhaps his attendance, and we might want to effect some discreet intervention. Or, if the kid has been a bit of a problem in the past for us, it might be the proverbial straw on the proverbial camel's back. We might profess righteous indignation and give him the push. The parents wouldn't object too strongly because they wouldn't want the dirty deed to be made public. So the files with this kind of information are kept under lock and key. In fact, they're in a fire-proof vault in the principal's office. There's stuff in there that could destroy the careers of more than one corporate nabob, let me tell you."

"And there's one of these files on Sloane?"

"There is, yes."

"Well, I'd like to see it. Would you mind?"

"I wouldn't mind in the least, but there's no way I can get it for you now, not without going through the principal, and he wouldn't release it without a court order, and that could cause immeasurable difficulties for me. The principal, not to mention the board of governors, would want to know how you knew that such a file existed. You see?"

Stark held his palms up.

"I do, yes. But—" He sighed. "—this is a murder

investigation, and if there's information that might help us, then I'm afraid that while you've been really cooperative and the last thing I want to do is to compromise you, but—"

Shapton raised a hand in a reassuring gesture.

"I'm actually trying to make things easier for you." She leaned forward. "I like a little scandal to shake the old boys up." She winked. "But if you go to the principal, he'll circle the wagons. Reputation here is everything. He'll block you at every path. However, there is a way I can get the information for you. I have a key to the vault, and I know where to find the skeletons, but I'll have to wait until everyone has left for the day before I go in there. So, if you don't mind, perhaps I could meet you later, off campus, if that's all right?"

"Yes, sure. I could come to your place if you like."

"Mmm. Why don't I meet you somewhere? What area do you live in?"

"I'm in the Beaches."

"Oh, I'm not far from there. That's fine. Is there somewhere—?"

"Well there's a local place that I—sometimes go," Stark said with a slightly sheepish smile. "It's called Carbo's. Here, I'll write the address for you. And here's my card. I'll put my home number and cell number on it, just in case. Okay?"

"Fine, I'll see you at, what? Eight o'clock?"

"Perfect."

****

Noel Harris went to visit Alan Sloane's sister, Nancy, with a last name he was unsure how to pronounce: Kuncevicius. Noel's boyfriend, Ernie Kowalski, helped with the pronunciation. He told him it was a Lithuanian name. It must have been a rich Lithuanian Nancy Sloane married, judging by the small mansion that presented itself at the address on a street off Russell Hill Road. Perhaps a nervous Lithuanian, since Harris was prevented by high, businesslike iron gates from driving into the curved driveway that ran under a broad *porte-cochère.*

He pressed a button on an intercom box, and an impatient male answered. After Harris gave his name and details, he had to wait for some time before the gates swung open. He parked under the overhang at the main door, and had to wait again after he rang the bell. He wondered whether he had been expected to use the service entrance. The woman who answered was somewhere in her mid-forties to mid-fifties, Harris reckoned. He assumed she was the housekeeper. She wore an unremarkable outfit of a grey wool skirt and navy sweater. Her face was drawn and tired. He was surprised to find that this was Nancy Kuncevicius, and a little embarrassed that his pronunciation of her name, which she corrected, was off the mark, but pleased that it wasn't too far off. He was wrong in his assumption that she had married into wealth. The house had been her parents'.

"We moved back in after they were killed. I apologize for the gate business. It's a holdover from my parent's time. My father had international business interests and was active in diplomatic circles. They often had foreign dignitaries staying with them. Hence the rather extensive security provisions. Since my husband died, I began locking the gate again. I'm a little nervous these days."

Harris nodded.

"Of course, I don't mean to be indelicate or intrusive, but you said your parents were—killed?"

"Yes, it was a hit-and-run accident Muskoka. A stolen car forced them off the road, and they tumbled into a steep ravine. They never did find the person who had been driving the stolen car. They found the car in Gravenhurst—but not him."

"I'm sorry. That's a terrible thing."

"Yes. And now this—Alan."

"Yes. It must be very hard on you. I'm really sorry."

"Well—" She sighed. "How can I help you? I've already spoken to two detectives. And I don't mind telling you that they were an objectionable pair." She gave him a weak smile. "You seem more considerate and a good deal more sensitive."

"Yes, we're not all—" He completed the sentence by a meaningful shrug.

"No," she said and waited.

"Right. Okay, I'm wondering whether your brother ever mentioned the names Corbett Chesley or Nigel Hawley?"

She pursed her lips and shook her head. "Not that I remember. Why?"

"They went to school with your brother.''

"I'm afraid I don't know much about that time of Alan's life. I'm ten years older than Alan. I'd already moved out when he was eight. My father and I didn't see eye-to-eye on many things. He thought I was flighty, not interested in serious matters. I liked dancing, and, while I don't look it now, I was a bit bohemian." She gave a little smile. "I was a folk singer. At least, l thought I was. In any case, I don't know much about my brother's adolescence, or even his young adulthood. My father doted on him. I know he forgave him any transgressions. He even brushed aside his homosexuality as being of no consequence."

Harris gave a half-smile.

"So, anything about that or my brother's private life I can't help you with. The other two asked the most tasteless questions about my brother's sexuality. I believe they suspect he was killed in a sort of lovers' tryst," she said with apparent distaste.

"But you don't"

"I have no idea."

"Is there anything about your brother's background that you think might help? Anything you can remember. Somebody who might have some animosity toward him?"

She shook her head.

"I can't help you. I'm sorry. I'm not concerned about scandal or anything like that. It's just that I don't know."

"Well, thank you. If you do think of anything, please give me a call." He handed her one of his cards.

****

Stark didn't immediately recognize the stunning woman with the flowing black hair who came into Carbo's that evening as waited for Diane Shapton. His eyes widened as the woman came and sat beside him. His memory picture of Shapton was of a reasonably attractive, fairly businesslike woman, not the angel on the next stool, an angel singing his name.

"My God," Stark said, sliding off his stool to his feet.

"Did I startle you?"

"No. It's just—I didn't—you've had your hair

done—or something. I didn't recognize you. It's a bit dark in here."

Her smile betrayed her amusement at Stark's bemusement.

"I try to leave the school-marm look at the college."

"Yeah, well you've been successful." He pulled out a stool for her. "Please." he said. "What can I get you to drink? Oh, let me introduce you. This is Morty Greenwood, the best piano-bar man east of the moon and west of the sun. Morty, this is Diane Shapton."

"How do you do," Morty said. "I see now why he's been drinking soda water."

"Oh, he has? Well, perhaps that's what I'll have."

"Oh, no, please. Have something stronger. I think I'll have a Scotch myself. What would you like?"

"Campari and soda, please."

Stark nodded slowly. "Okay. Don't move. I'll be right back."

"So," Shapton said as Stark went to the bar, "I get the impression Mr. Stark is something of a regular here?"

"Harold? When he shuffles off his mortal coil, they're going to have his barstool bronzed. May I play something for you?"

"What's his favourite song?"

"Oh, he's got a lot of them. But most of them are pretty heavy. I'm supposed to play dinner music sort of stuff at this time of the evening, on the orders of our beloved leader, Ulysses, who owns the place and is leaning on the end of the bar over there, looking at you and drooling on his shirt front."

"Morty, you're embarrassing me."

"I'll play 'The Nearness of You'."

Stark returned with the drinks.

"Has Morty been entertaining you? Nice tune."

"The lady's request," Morty said.

Stark smiled broadly. "Oh, is that so? Good taste, too. Well, cheers."

"Cheers."

They took a table in a corner. They chatted about novels and poetry and Shakespeare. She was polite and refrained from correcting him more than once. Stark began to realize he was out of his depth, and changed the subject to his favourite diatribe on the deterioration of the English language. He was pleased that she agreed with him that the school curriculum would do well to return to teaching the basics of grammar, but that most teachers younger than she were ill-equipped to teach the subject. However, once again, Stark's views on the issue were superficial and simplistic, while she spoke from experience and considerable knowledge of pedagogy. Stark was anxious, talking a lot, almost babbling. He was at once excited and intimidated by her intelligence, and found himself trying too hard to impress her. Realizing this, and at the risk of sounding patronizing, she asked him about his work as a policeman. He became immediately laconic, and quickly changed the subject. That stirred her curiosity, and eventually she returned to the topic. He became terse again, and at last she said, "Are you not happy being a detective?"

"Happy? Happiness is not a condition I seek in my work. I like to solve puzzles. I get a certain satisfaction out of that. I enjoy it, but it doesn't make me happy."

"You don't feel good about making the world safer, about bringing criminals to book, providing justice to the victims and their families?"

He leaned toward her.

"Frankly, I don't give a flying—I don't give a damn about the victims. In fact, I have no use for cops who see themselves as avenging angels."

"You think they're hypocrites?"

"No, I don't think they're hypocrites. I think they're unprofessional. And dangerous. Since you've opened this can of worms, I think there are two kinds of very dangerous police officers. The first is the kind I've alluded to, who take on the roles of prosecutor, judge and jury, and sometimes—though, thank God, very rarely—executioner. They're dangerous not only because they're usurping authority, but also because their zeal muddies their judgement. The second kind is the totally self-serving cop who acts only in the interest of his own advancement. Both kinds present a serious risk of gross injustice, of bending the rules to get a result. And both—their ability to reason being seriously compromised—are quite capable of nabbing the wrong person and letting the guilty one go free." Stark became aware that he had been leaning farther and farther over the table. He sat back in his chair with a laugh. "Why did I let you get me on to this? It's not a good subject for me. Not a good subject."

"I'm sorry. Weird weather we're having, eh?" She grinned, and Stark smiled and nodded. "History. What about history?" she said.

"What about it?"

"As a subject."

"History's good. Would you like another cognac?"

"Oh, no thanks. I've had too much already."

"Right." Stark leaned back, patted his stomach, and then self-consciously sat up straight again, pulling his gut in. "Well, I hate to bring it up, and I don't want to cut the evening short, believe me, but maybe we could talk about the purpose of our meeting?"

"Ah, yes, the file."

"Did you get it?"

"Oh, I got it. Yes." She looked around. "The thing is, I'm not sure this is the best sort of venue in which to be examining and discussing a confidential document."

Stark looked around.

"No? Well—"

"I take it you don't live far from here?"

"I'm just down the street," Stark said quickly, his heart racing.

"If I'm not being too forward, perhaps we could repair to your drawing room, as they say. I could do with some coffee."

"Sure—it's a bit of a mess, I'm afraid. I live alone—"

She nodded. "Yes, something about you told me you were unattached."

"Oh?"

"Don't worry about your place. It can't be any worse than my dump."

Stark nodded slowly.

"Oh, yes, it can. Anyway, sure, let's go."

Stark stood up, almost knocking over his chair.

"The bill. Don't you think we should—"

"I already signed. I'll take care of it later."

"I insist on paying for mine. I couldn't possibly let you—"

"The department'll take care of it. I'll put you down as an informant."

"Oh, thanks a lot."

****

A white blur shot past from the living room toward

the bedroom as they entered the apartment.

"What the hell was that?" Shapton said.

"That was Powder, the closet cat. She doesn't like people. She barely tolerates me. She spends about seventy-five per cent of the time in the closet in my room. And one hundred per cent of the time in there if there's anyone with me in the apartment."

"My God. What's she so frightened of?"

"Oh, years ago I brought a dog home, when she was fairly young, and the dog terrorized her. It traumatized her. She's never been normal since."

"Poor thing."

"Ah, she has the run of the place when I'm not here. And when I am here, I'm nearly always alone."

"I see."

"I'm not fishing for sympathy. I like it that way. I like it just fine that way." He made a sweeping motion with his hand. "It means I don't have to worry about the mess—well, except at times like this. I did warn you that it was a disaster area. I'm sorry."

"Looks fine to me," she lied.

Stark made coffee. They sat at the kitchen table.

"Do you mind?" she said, holding up a pack of unfiltered Camels.

"Of course not," said Stark, taking a pack of Gauloises from his pocket and showing her. She laughed. "I have to say, you're the first woman I've met who's smoked Camels."

"Shameless, isn't it? I spent some time in Europe and got used to their rather strong cigarettes. I'd probably be smoking your Gauloises, but I didn't know you could buy them here."

"In that case, have one of mine. I get them from a

store downtown. I'll write down the name and address for you.'' Stark lit her cigarette and his own. "I'm impressed. I like people who march to their own drummer."

"Good," she said, smiling. "So do I. Here." She took a file folder out of her attaché case and placed it in front of Stark. He looked at her and opened the file. It contained a single sheet of paper, typed, single-spaced, type produced by a typewriter, not a computer printer.

"Typewriter. Looks funny today. You know, with computers. I learned typing in high school. I felt really modern with that, superior. My handwriting is so bad. Now, this stuff looks—primitive, dark ages. Things have changed so much. Whoever typed this was dyslexic. Full of transpositions. Word missing here, I think. Somebody in a hurry, maybe. Who would have typed it?"

"Perhaps the headmaster at the time. I don't recall who it was. Do you need to know that?"

"No. Not at this point. Interesting reading. Who was this Master Edward Blaide? One of the students?"

"No, we call the teachers masters, like the English system, although we use principal, rather than headmaster."

"Master Blaide was a teacher? So, where would this information have come from? Holy cow—have you read this?"

"Yes, of course. It jogged my memory. Of course, at the time, I was a teacher, so I wasn't privy to that kind of information officially, but the rumour was that they had hired a private detective, and the report reads that way, don't you think?"

"Yeah. That's what I wondered. My God. There he is. There they are. All three of them. You didn't remember this? It must have been a big scandal."

Shapton shook her head vigorously. "No. It was all hushed up. I suspect, in fact I'm almost sure, the parents weren't even told."

"I can see that, witchcraft in one of the bastions of old morality. Old fairies diddling the young boys would be an anticipated risk, especially among those fathers who themselves had attended a similar institution. Not desirable, but it wouldn't make you pregnant. But witchcraft. Oh no. Not good at all."

"I think they would have spoken to the boys, being careful not to be specific about the misdeed, in order to be able to deny precise knowledge of what was going on if parents later did get wind of it, but leaving no doubt among the boys that both their ceasing the behaviour alluded to and their silence vis-a-vis their parents were required in order to avoid dire consequences. You mention the diddling. It's funny, because I remember that that was what we thought it was all about with young Sloane, who displayed tendencies in that direction from the beginning. In fact, we thought it might well have been Sloane who had led Blaide astray and not the other way around. We had no knowledge of the involvement of the other two. I had no idea that they were part of it until I read this report today."

"So, this Blaide was part of some sort of coven. Look at this, 'nude rituals.' Actually, it's been typed 'nude r-i-t-a-u-l-s.' It says Blaide's resignation was going to be demanded and he would be asked to sign a declaration that he would not hold the school liable nor reveal any of the goings-on. There was no declaration in the file?"

"Blaide probably refused to sign it. If he had half a

brain he would have. They would have offered him money and then threatened to withhold it, but he'd know they wouldn't take the chance of pushing him out broke and full of resentment. They'd have paid him off out of operating funds to avoid having to inform the board. And they would have given him a letter of recommendation. We were told he left for medical reasons."

"Well. We've got to find Master Edward Blaide. And the quicker the better. I get the impression you don't know what happened to him?"

"I can probably find out."

"How quickly can you find out?"

"I'm not sure. If he remained a teacher, maybe fifteen minutes, maybe two minutes."

"Right now?"

"No-no. It would have to be tomorrow morning."

"What time? You'd have to go into school to do it?"

"Eight-thirty. Are you on the Internet? You have a computer here?"

"Yes—both."

"Well, I could do it from here."

Stark looked at her, and she looked back, unblinking.

****

Noel Harris was dispatched to West Toronto Secondary School with orders to find and follow Edward Blaide. The board's security officer had wanted to know why the police were interested in the teacher, who was actually retired, but was working on contract because, as a music specialist, he was in demand. When Harris told the security officer it was a routine matter, and nothing he need to be concerned about, he accepted the fact that he wasn't going to be given any further details. He provided a fairly recent photograph of Blaide and even met Harris at the school and escorted him to Blaide's classroom, where Harris was able to see the teacher through the window in the door.

Harris waited in the parking lot in his ancient yellow Volvo until he saw Blaide emerge. He followed him to a three-storey house on Harbord Street, each floor of which was a flat. Blaide had the downstairs apartment.

That evening, he followed Blaide to the Norval Furs building on Spadina Avenue. All the floors above the first were offices, with a diverse assortment of occupants, according to the list on the wall of the lobby. They included three labour unions; a couple of detective agencies; various associations, among which were the Organization for Progressive Anarchy and the Theurgical Society, which was listed beside the number thirty-one. It was through the door of office thirty-one that Harris heard what sounded like a group of people chanting. Since a quick run along the corridors of the floor above revealed no signs of life, Harris thought it was a fair assumption that Blaide was in thirty-one, although he had no idea what theurgical meant.

The meeting in office thirty-one continued until 10:37 p.m., at which time Harris followed Blaide home, with a stop at Fran's on College Street, where Blaide ordered a hamburger, fries and coleslaw to go and had a coffee while he waited. Theurgicalling must give you an appetite, Harris thought. After the lights went out in Blaide's apartment, about twelve-fifteen, and without specific instructions to the contrary from Stark, Harris went home. There, he consulted a dictionary and the Internet.

****

"Theurgy. It's mumbo-jumbo. White magic, calling on beneficent deities. It's witchcraft, I guess," Harris told Stark on the phone.

"So why'd you break off surveillance?"

"Ah, Jesus, Sarge, I wasn't going to stay there all night."

"I'm kidding. So this outfit, does it have a phone number?"

"The Theurgical Society?"

"Yeah."

"I doubt it."

"Well, have a look."

"All right. Just a minute." Harris got the phone book and flipped through it. "Geez, it's here all right. But I can't imagine there'd be anybody at the place during the day. It's in this rundown building on Spadina. They probably just rent the space for their meetings. Anyway, what do you want the number for?"

"I don't want it. You do."

"Me? What do I want it for?"

"Because you're going to join the group."

"Join the group? Wait a minute. If this guy is the killer, well, Jesus, shouldn't we be calling in the whole crew about now? We've got the three victims tied together and we've got this guy right in the picture."

"As what?"

"As the killer."

"Get out of here. All we have is a connection among the four of them, and that was twenty-four years ago, for Pete's sake. Why would the guy wait twenty-four years to kill them? And why kill them?"

"You're the one—"

"Hold it. I didn't say there wasn't the beginning of

a possibility that this looney-tune might have been ordered by the avenging angel of Isis to turn the three of them into sacrifices. There's also a possibility that the three never left the magic circle. But the point is, we don't have any more than that."

"But what if the guy is a serial killer?"

"I don't think that that's what this is, and besides, if he is, he's got another two weeks and three days before he's scheduled to do his next murder. So, I want you to join this group."

"They're not going to just let me join. What do I say? 'Gee, I just got into town and I was looking for a local theurgy group to join'."

"No no no. You've got to play a bit of a role here, Harris. You've got to play the part of a new-age hippie, you know, crystals and pyramids and white witches and amulets. You just slur your words, pretend your IQ is about ninety. You should be able to pull that off."

"This is ridiculous."

"No, it's not, and listen. Your hair."

"What about my hair?"

"It doesn't look like a hippie's hair. It looks like a cop's hair."

"Well I guess it would. What am I supposed to do about it?"

"Shave it off."

"Forget it."

"They won't believe you—"

"I'm not shaving my head on the chance that they'll let me in."

"All right, wear a hat."

****

Harris phoned the number and got an answering

machine. He left his number and waited. At four-fifteen in the afternoon, the phone rang.

"Is Claude there, please?" It was an older man's voice, perhaps Blaide.

"Yeah, dis is Claude." Noel tried to sound half-stoned.

Chapter Seven

"'Sweet Thursday'. Arrived in the mail this morning," Ted Henry said. "What do you think it means, Harry?"

"Well, it's the title of a book by John Steinbeck. As I recall, it doesn't have any meaning except Sweet Thursday followed Lousy Wednesday."

"What do you think this means?"

With a pair of tweezers, Henry held up the sheet of white bond on which were pasted the words 'Sweet Thursday', which appeared to have been clipped from different parts of a newspaper.

"Well, I imagine it's our guy."

"Exactly. Sending us a message. I think I should go to the inspector with this."

"Wait, Ted. We've got a guy. We've found a connection among the three victims. The three of them attended Thomas Cranmer College at exactly the same time."

"Jesus."

"And the three were implicated in some kind of witchcraft thing that a teacher was involved in."

"Holy shit."

"The teacher was given the boot, but we've found him again, and he's still into this stuff. I've got Harris infiltrating the organization."

"That could be bloody dangerous."

"Harris lives for danger."

"I never got that impression."

"No? Well, anyway, he's joining the group. We're keeping very close tabs on this fellow."

"God, if this guy does another killing while we've got him in our sights, they'll crucify me."

"We haven't got enough—we haven't got anything, really, to bring the guy in on. And it could be the old feral fowl pursuit."

"What the hell's that?"

"Wild goose chase."

"Well, don't let this guy out of your sight. I think I'd better give you a couple of more officers."

Stark sighed. "Plainclothes constables. I don't want any Homicide dicks on this. And just two. We'll spell them off. And don't tell them a thing. They're just to keep an eye on the guy. Okay?"

"Yeah, fine. Give me the details. And you'd better get that paper to forensics."

****

If there were going to be any nude prancing at the Theurgical Society meeting, Noel Harris wasn't looking forward to it. Apart from the fact they were draped in white robes and had amulets hanging from their necks on gold chains, and plastic flowers in their hair (they used real wildflowers in season, it was explained), this bunch could have been a Weight Watchers group. The only one who seemed to be under two hundred pounds was Edward Blaide, the Mage, as he was known, and one woman with the body of a garden rake.

If you addressed the Mage, you were to speak reverently, with head bowed, and call him (at your choice) O Great One, O Glorious Leader, O Wondrous

One, O Sage, O Wise One, and some other titles Harris had forgotten. You were to obey him implicitly.

"He would never ask you to jump out the window," the short, round woman, who looked like a snowman in her white outfit, explained to Harris earnestly. "But if he did, you'd have to obey."

"Like wow. I can dig it. Right on," Harris said idiotically, feeling more of a fool than he must have appeared, because the snow-woman seemed to be impressed. Blaide had yet to make his appearance as the Mage. He had been the one who had responded to Harris's phone message. He had asked the policeman a long list of questions, most of which were either patently transparent in their purpose or had been cunningly crafted by an expert to trick respondents into betraying their true motives. Harris thought the former situation must have obtained. He had given answers that had revealed him as a lost soul, aimless, rather stupid, easily led, eager to submit to a guiding hand, gullible and willing to believe in anything—from voices of the dead to visitors from outer space. Blaide had told him there was a meeting every night of the week at the building on Spadina, but that members were expected to attend only two meetings a week, while he, the leader, was present nearly every night and would be that evening and that if he, Claude, chose to present himself, he would be welcomed, and a mentor would be assigned to him to provide a preliminary orientation. At a certain point in the evening, he would be asked to leave, which procedure would be followed until he was formally initiated into the circle, with all attendant rights, privileges, delights and benefits.

Looking at his fellow theurgists, Harris couldn't

imagine anything that might constitute a delight. In the phone conversation, Blaide had not struck him as a powerful personality, but when the man entered the room that night, wearing a long, red robe with the encircled five-pointed star of the pentacle and the mask of Anubis, the Egyptian jackal god responsible for the preservation of the dead, he made an imposing figure. Something in the mask amplified his voice. It was resonant, deep and mesmerizing. After some initial bowing and sign-making, Harris's guide gently pushed him away from the group as a circle was swept with a crudely made broom and each of the group entered the swept area from the same point, the Mage placing a black mark on their foreheads with a stick. They walked around the circle until all of them had entered. Blaide said some words over a bowl of what looked like salt and a glass pitcher of water on a small altar. He mixed them together and chanted, "As the two are mixed, they become neither salt nor water, but the fluid of life." He then carried the mixture around the circle and sprinkled it on the floor. He repeated the circling with a stick of incense. The Mage then walked around the circle with a double-edged knife. He chanted, "Hail to the guardians of the north, powers of earth and healing. Lend us your stability and your strength in our circle this night."

He went through a similar routine with the east, south and west. Various other chants and invocations followed, and then Harris was ushered to the door.

"So, what happened?"

Stark yawned as if he weren't interested in Harris's answer. He rubbed his face with both hands, shook his head, spread his eyes vertically with his fingers on his forehead and thumbs on a cheek bone. Sid Holtzman and

Harris gave each other self-righteously disapproving looks.

"What happened?" Stark repeated, half-turning toward Harris when he didn't immediately respond.

"Well, it was a witch thing, sort of. It was a whole bunch of pagan religions mixed together, Egyptian, Wicca, Norse, you name it. They didn't do much—a bunch of chanting, formed a circle which I wasn't permitted to join, being not a full initiate. It's a pretty harmless-looking group, about half a dozen women and four men, not including me and the great white leader, who's actually a red leader."

"Red leader," Sid said. "I heard that in a war movie the other night—fighter pilots. The one guy was Red Leader. Isn't that funny—"

"Sid," Stark said. "Don't speak. And what are you doing standing there listening? This is police business. Go to the other end of the counter."

"You go to the other end of the counter. This is my place, for Pete's sake. The breakfast rush is over, but pretty soon, the coffee-break crowd will start coming in. Go sit in the back booth and close the door, you don't want me to listen. Go to your office, you want to talk private. Police business." Sid began furiously polishing the glass doors on the dessert cooler.

"Just don't interrupt. Go on," Stark said to Harris.

"The guy wore this long red robe and a big jackal mask."

"Jackal? Scary?"

"Imposing. Made his voice echo. Weird stuff. You could see how vulnerable people would be easily impressed and influenced by a guy like that. And yet when I talked to him on the phone, he was meek and mild."

"Obviously you had no trouble talking yourself into the group."

"I got the impression they were glad to see me. I guess they're always looking for new blood," Harris said blood melodramatically. "He asked a bunch of rather obvious questions, and I gave him a bunch of stock answers. I'm supposed to be from Timmins, and I'm supposed to be searching for meaning in my life."

"Do you know anybody in Timmins?"

"I don't even know where it is."

"So, what else happened?"

"Nothing. Maybe something more ominous later, but before the good stuff got started, I had to leave.''

Stark's head snapped around.

"Did you have a heavy date or something?"

"They told me at the start that at a certain point, I wouldn't be allowed to stay because I'm not initiated."

"That's probably when they plan the ritual murders."

"I can't imagine it. But listen, who were the two cops?"

"Cops?"

"Outside, behind the building in the parking lot. Klutzes. They stood out like sore thumbs."

"They weren't supposed to be there. I told them to go to the guy's apartment. I figured you'd follow him after the meeting."

"You didn't tell me to do that."

"Jesus. Don't you have any initiative?"

"I guess not. In any case, these two were a real pair. They were in an unmarked car, an old Camaro. I came ambling around the corner of the building, and I saw them right away in the far corner of the lot. Big signs say private, unauthorized vehicles will be towed and like that, but Blaide told me it was okay to park there after seven. So, I came around the corner, and they saw me and ducked down. It was like the Keystone Kops. What's going on?"

"They were supposed to go to Blaide's apartment building."

"It's a house."

"When I told Henry we had a line on the guy who might be doing these killings, he insisted on giving us help. He doesn't want Blaide wandering around unescorted killing off more citizens."

"He wants him to have an escort for his murders?"

"You're not funny. These two plainclothes constables know nothing about why they're supposed to watch Blaide, just that they're supposed to watch him, and we'll spell them off."

"When are you going to take your shift?"

"I'm the brains."

Harris shook his head.

"We're all in trouble," Sid put in.

"I told you to keep quiet." Stark said.

"You'd better give me the names and numbers of these two so I can contact them and arrange a schedule," Harris said. "And I guess you want me to keep going to the coven, or whatever it is?"

Stark's cell phone rang. He answered and his eyes widened. He jumped off his stool and took a seat in a booth, huddling against the window.

Sid smiled.

"That's a good sign."

"What?"

"Well, look at him. Who do you think's on the other end of the line?"

"You think it might be Carol Weems?"

Sid shook his head. "Doubt that. It's a woman, that's for sure. Be wonderful if it was Weems, but any woman would be good. Christ, unless it is Weems and she gives him a boot in the heart. No, he's smiling. It's okay."

Stark pressed the end button on the phone and got up from the booth. He was beaming, gazing into the distance, his thoughts a long way off. When he returned from his reverie, he saw Holtzman and Harris looking at him.

"What the hell are you staring at?"

Diane Shapton had arranged to have dinner with him. Chinese food, and they were going to order it in at his place.

****

As soon as the rain stopped, the temperature fell. For a brief time, everything smelled dank of wet, rotting leaves, and then it got too cold to smell. Toward the end of the day, it started to snow: nothing serious, just a few tentative flakes, some of which clung to Diane Shapton's hair like sparkles on black velvet. Stark thought that if it were possible, the woman was even more attractive in jeans and an oversized roll-neck sweater in teal blue than she had been the other night in the high-fashion dress. He had already decided she must spend considerable time in the gym. It was difficult to imagine that her next big stop would be sixty, but she had such a classically beautiful face, he figured she would be alluring at seventy-five, pulling sixty-year-olds who'd think her twenty years younger.

"How are you doing with the case?"

100

"Oh, fine. Yeah, very good. What can I get you to drink?"

"Nothing, thanks, I'm fine. And Blaide? Were you able to track him down?"

Stark hesitated, and then, apologetically, as if he were asking her forgiveness, he said, "I can't speak about that, Diane. I'm sorry."

"I understand. I just hope I was helpful."

"You were, yes. Very helpful. Thank you."

She gave him an arch look.

"I meant about the case."

"What? Oh yeah, right. No, I was talking about the case, but you were very helpful in other ways, too, although I don't think I'd use the term 'helpful' in that regard. So, do you want to listen to some music?"

"How about a video?"

"A video?"

"Yes. You do have a VCR?"

Stark looked around automatically, as if trying to remember whether he had such a thing.

"Oh sure, yes. I have one." He pointed to it.

"I see it, yes." She nodded as though talking to a little boy. "Do you watch movies?"

"Oh, sure. There's a place just down the street. Do you want to get a movie? C'mon, we'll go down there."

"No, I'll wait here."

"I won't know what to get."

"I'm sure your taste will be impeccable. Surprise me."

"You like swamp creature movies?"

"Love 'em."

"Well, you're not getting one."

She laughed. "Oh, okay."

"I'll be right back. The CD player's there. Make yourself a drink. I won't be long."

Stark returned with *Chinatown*.

"I thought it would go with the food."

"Excellent choice. It's one of my very favourites."

"Great, now what kind of Chinese food do you like?—"

They made love twice during the night, and once in the morning. Stark should have been exhausted, but since he had had only two glasses of wine, he felt better than he did most mornings.

Over toast and coffee, she asked him whether she could have the addresses of Corbett Chesley and Nigel Hawley.

"They were former students, and I think it's only right that I offer the condolences of the school and my personal sympathy. It generally falls to the associate principal to do these things."

"Well, I don't know. Yeah, I guess that's not a problem, Carol."

"Carol?"

"What did I say?"

"You said, Carol. Thanks a lot. Who's Carol?"

Chapter Eight

It was late in the season for rock climbing, but in the last few days, the cold, wet weather had vanished as quickly as it had come, and the freak balminess had returned as November eased into December. Bruce Anderton was addicted to the sport. And climbing helped him think. He needed time to think about what he had found and what to do about it, especially since he had begun to realize, reluctantly, that it might involve someone he had trusted all his life. And so he had come to this spot near Bracebridge, where, years before, he had discovered an isolated cliff deep in the bush, a site you had to walk in to, a site that couldn't be seen from any road or waterway. He parked his Mercedes four-by-four on the roadside, took the long climbing rope out of the back of the vehicle, and draped it over one shoulder and across his body obliquely. He fastened on his climbing belt, pulled on his boots, and began to trek into the bush. It took him an hour to climb the rock face. It was only eighteen metres high, but the surface was smooth, with few handholds, and Anderton tried to avoid using pitons. He preferred a natural climb.

There wasn't much of a view from the top. Most of the height of the rock was accounted for by a depression at its base, so you walked downhill when approaching the foot of the rock. The configuration of the terrain meant that the top of the rock wasn't much higher than the surrounding thickly treed landscape, which was the main reason the spot was relatively unknown. Anderton sat atop the rock thinking about who had taken him to it years before. He thought about what he was going to do about the situation and finally reached the decision he had known all along he was going to have to come to in the end. He would have to go to the police.

Resigned to that course of action, he methodically hooked up his rope for the rappel and began his descent. The instant his head disappeared below the top of the rock, a serrated knife blade was sawn across the taut rope, rapidly cutting through the strands. The rope shot over the edge. It was not a long fall. Anderton spent less than two seconds of his descent wondering what had happened. He had no time to scream.

****

With the weather's sudden change for the better, and because he was feeling so good about life, Stark decided he would take a stake-out shift after all. He replaced Harris in the school parking lot at eleven in the morning, and realized his timing had been bad when the students came lurching and swaying and strutting out of the building at lunchtime and all but destroyed his mood.

"Louts."

A group of them climbed into a battered old Honda at the other end of the lot, and played the radio. Stark's car vibrated with the thump-thump-thump.

"Mindless. They're bloody mindless."

After school, he followed Blaide home. Eventually, Stark was replaced by Harris in his yellow Volvo. On principle, and just to keep his reputation intact, he called Harris on his cell phone. "The guy's going to recognize that goddamned car of yours. It stands out like a sore

104

thumb, for God's sake. Tomorrow, ask Henry to let you have an undercover car. Jesus."

****

The following morning, Stark got a call from Ted Henry.

"There's been another one."

"Another what?"

"Another killing."

"What makes you think it was one of ours?"

"Yesterday was Thursday."

"But it hasn't been a month yet. And it couldn't have been Blaide. We've had him under constant surveillance."

"Slow down. I got another note this morning. Came by courier. It says, 'Thursday sweet in Muskoka heart even not a month apart.'"

"A frigging poet. What's Muskoka got to do with it?"

"There was a murder near Bracebridge yesterday. A rock climber. Guy was climbing alone up a steep cliff, and somebody cut the rope. The guy was younger than the others, only thirty. Successful. He was a forensic accountant. Worked on his own, a consultant, which is why he could go rock-climbing in the middle of the week."

"And don't tell me."

"What?"

"He was a graduate of Cranmer College."

"He was."

"C'mon, Ted. How would you know that?"

"He was wearing a graduation ring."

Stark took a deep breath and let it out. "Whatdya know."

"The OPP—"

"Ah Jesus. Don't tell me I have to work with those jerks."

"They're good policemen, Stark. I was going to say that they're happy to let us have the case. They've done a thoroughly professional job at the scene, and they'll let us have their report and the forensics, but from what they told me, there doesn't seem to be anything of much use there. The rope appeared to have been cut with a serrated blade. It had to be very sharp. This climbing rope is tough. Made like that so it doesn't get frayed against sharp rocks. They figure the knife might even be a really expensive kitchen knife. I told them we have a suspect, and that we've got evidence to tie the killing to an ongoing investigation. So it's all ours."

"And I don't have to go up to Muskoka?"

"No. I'm going to have to bring everybody in on this now. I'll have to tell Peters. God. He's going to have a shit haemorrhage."

"No-no, wait."

"I can't hold off any longer, Stark. Jesus."

"One night. I want to try something before everything gets too legal."

"Too legal? Wait a minute—"

"One more night."

"I can't, Harry."

Stark sighed. "All right, then you don't know where I am. And don't tell him about Blaide. Not yet. I'm being a secretive prick as usual, I've gone undercover and I haven't given you a full report yet. Tomorrow, I'll show up and fill him in. Idiot."

"Who?"

"Peters. How about it, Ted?"

Henry sighed. "You're not going to try to beat a confession out of the guy?"

"I just want to check something out, that's all. Before the big feet and the big mouths and the heavy hands get in there. All right?"

"One night."

"That's all I need, Ted. So who was the dead guy?"

"His name was Bruce Anderton. He lives, get this, on the Bridle Path."

"Forensic accountancy must be a lucrative racket."

"It turns out he inherited the joint from his old man, who was, literally, an old man. He died not too long ago, at eighty-two. So he was about fifty-two when the son was born. The mother died years ago, when the son was a kid."

"The kid lived alone in a mansion on the Bridle Path?

"He wasn't married. I can tell you that. They didn't say he lived with anyone."

"Big old house. Great spot for a witches' saturnalia, wouldn't you say?"

"There's a butler, a sort of houseman, looks after the place. The provincials sent somebody around. I guess you'd better start there."

****

The freakish weather made another sharp turn, and it was raining heavily by the time Stark got to the Anderton house. The wind was whipping sheets of water across the windshield, defeating the wipers' efforts to keep the glass clear. Had the conditions been different, Stark might have recognized the house as one he had visited in the past. He parked beside the building, behind a Range Rover. Ahead of that, the garage door was open, and Stark could see the unmistakable rear of a gleaming, rather ancient, black Rolls-Royce.

Stark had to wait for some time after pressing the doorbell button, which produced a sound like a Chinese gong. The man who finally answered the door was wearing black serge trousers, a white shirt and a black-and-silver-striped tie. He was tall, in his early sixties maybe, Stark figured, ramrod straight, broad-shouldered and with a flat stomach. His hair was black, with grey at the temples, and cut short. His face was unlined and expressionless.

"Yes?"

Stark showed his badge.

"Detective Stark—say, don't I recognize you? Wait a minute, I've been here before."

The butler spoke almost without intonation.

"You were here last summer. Briefly. You asked to see Mr. Anderton Senior, and when I told you he had passed away, you uttered an epithet and left without explanation."

"That's right. It was when the old jewellery courier got killed, and I found out Anderton owned the building where it took place. Now I remember. You mind if I come in?"

The butler stood aside, and Stark entered. He had put on an Irish slouch hat against the rain. The butler held out his hand for the hat as Stark passed.

"That's all right," Stark said, whacking the water off the hat against his raincoat. "I'll keep it. I always forget the damned things if I put them down. Where can we sit?"

The butler indicated a door on the left of the cavernous foyer. The plain Georgian exterior of the building had an unremarkable appearance and belied the size of the structure. A casual observer might not notice it was three storeys high and would not be aware that it was twice as deep as it was wide. Stark saw a similarity between the interior of the house and that of Cranmer College, with dark wood panels hung with paintings, although most of these were landscapes or still lifes, with a scattering of abstracts, and only one portrait.

"Is that the old man?" Stark asked.

"That is Horace Anderton."

"Miserable-looking old bugger. Where d'you want me to go?" The door gave entrance to the library, a large room with a ceiling as high as the entrance hall's, and lined, floor to ceiling, with books, many of them custom-bound. Stark pulled one from its shelf, a first edition of Vanity Fair. He was impressed and envious. He went to put the book back, and the butler took it from him and placed it carefully back on the shelf. The room was filled with heavy carved wood and leather furniture. Stark went to sit behind the wide desk, discovering a large, grey cat curled on the chair. He pushed the cat gently to the floor.

"Look out, puss."

The butler picked up the cat and stroked it, both he and the cat giving Stark a resentful look. Stark opened his notebook.

"What's your name?"

"Calvin Unger."

The butler remained standing, as if it weren't his place to sit down.

"Okay, Calvin Unger, how long have you been employed here? Why don't you sit?"

"Since 1952." He ignored Stark's suggestion.

"Jesus, that's a long time. Your whole working life?"

"Yes."

"And you're how old now?"

"Is that relevant?"

"No, I suppose not. So, who else lives here?"

"No one."

"No one? There was just you and the deceased—"

"Yes. Just the two of us."

"Big place for two people. I guess you'll be having to retire now, eh?"

"I wouldn't know."

"Well, I guess it depends on the person the house has been left to. Do you know who that would be?"

"No."

"There were no other children?"

"Mr. Anderton married late. He was fifty-one. His wife was much younger. She died of an aneurysm at the age of thirty-seven, when Master Bruce was six years of age. Mr. Anderton raised his son alone."

"What about brothers or sisters—of the old man I mean."

"He was an only child."

"Cousins or something?"

The butler sighed, betraying his feeling that having to explain these things to this vulgar person was an imposition.

"Mr. Anderton came to this country at the age of fifteen, from the Ukraine. He went to Saskatchewan, and worked on farms. A wealthy farmer adopted him, unofficially, and sent him to university. Eventually, Mr. Anderton became a stockbroker. He moved to Toronto and he changed his name. If there are any cousins, it will probably be impossible to trace them. That, however, will be up to the lawyers."

"I see. In the meantime, which could be a long, long time, you've got a rather big house all to yourself."

The butler didn't respond.

"Did young Bruce entertain here, particularly after his father died?"

"He occasionally had friends in."

"Recently?"

"He had a cocktail party about two months ago, but Master Bruce travelled a good deal on business. In the past two years, he was away much more than he was home."

"A cocktail party? Wild affairs, these cocktail parties?"

The butler shook his head firmly, gave Stark a look of indignation.

"No."

"Did he have a girlfriend—or a boyfriend?"

"He socialized with young women, but there was no one in particular."

"Drugs?"

"No," Unger said sharply.

"You seem very sure of that."

"Master Bruce was athletic—"

"That seems to have been his undoing."

"—He swam. There's a pool in the house. And he played squash, often with his father. There is a squash court in the house also, and a gymnasium."

"Good God."

"Mr. Anderton Senior provided Bruce with everything he needed. Because of his busy schedule, he was not always able to spend as much time as he would have liked with his son. He theorized that by stimulating a taste for physical activity, he might suppress deleterious habits. When possible, we were all involved in athletic pursuits along with Bruce."

"Well, it looks as if it's kept you fit."

"Yes."

"I wonder whether you're pre-empting my next question, which is, despite the efforts of his father, did Bruce become involved in any behaviour that one might characterize as—as you put it so well—deleterious?"

"No."

Stark raised a hand.

"Now, wait, Mr. Unger, please. I'm sure you feel it's your duty to protect the family name. But Bruce has been murdered. Finding his killer is more important than guarding his reputation. Did he take drugs, or gamble, or have any sexual peculiarities? Was he ever in any sort of trouble?"

"No."

"Okay, does that mean 'no', or you don't know?"

"It means 'no'."

"Somebody killed him, and it wasn't something that occurred at random. Somebody had to know where he was going to be and how to get there and had to be waiting for him. I've read the OPP report. The local detachment didn't even know this place where he fell existed. So somebody had to have a reason for killing him, don't you think?"

"I suppose so."

"Did he have any enemies, anyone who might want to kill him, anyone who might benefit from his death?"

"I'm not aware of anyone."

"He attended Thomas Cranmer College, didn't he?

He was wearing a ring."

"Yes."

"Did anything happen during his time at the school that might fit in the general category of scandal?"

The butler shook his head.

"Did he belong to any kind of club, or organization at the school?"

"He played sports, football, hockey and tennis."

"That's it?"

The butler shrugged. "Yes."

"He was a good student?"

"Top of his class."

"Okay." Stark stood and walked over to the bookshelves. He looked at the beautifully bound, beautiful things, and sighed.

"Bruce did forensic accounting, didn't he?"

"Yes."

"He was responsible for people's being arrested, going to jail, isn't that right?"

"He didn't discuss his work with me."

Stark half-turned to look at Unger.

"Yes, but that must have been what happened, eh?"

"I suppose so."

"So somebody might want to stop him from telling something that he knew that could get him or her into trouble with the law, wouldn't you think so?"

"As I said—"

Stark raised a hand to silence the rest of the remark.

"Okay. Where's his office?"

"I think I'd better call Mr. Anderton's lawyer."

"What for?"

"I don't think I can permit you to go through his private business papers. They may well contain confidential information."

"Yes, you're right. They may well. Call the lawyer if you want to, but if you don't show me where Bruce's office is, I'll start taking every room apart. I think you've lived in this rarefied atmosphere too long, Calvin. There's actually a real world out there."

The butler glared at Stark for a moment, and then led him across the foyer and through a door on the opposite side that led to a long corridor, ranged with doors. He opened the last door in the line. The room had a desk and a couple of leather-cushioned dark wooden armchairs, a matching filing cabinet and credenza. On the panelled wall, there was a single water colour of an uninteresting landscape. Every horizontal surface was bare.

"This was his office?"

"Yes."

"Where is everything? There's not even a pen on the desk."

"The Andertons were very neat. Master Bruce put everything away when he finished with it."

Stark pulled at the desk drawer.

"It's locked." He tried the filing cabinet and the credenza with the same result. "Where are the keys?"

"I would have no reason to have a key to Mr. Anderton's private papers."

"His keys will be downtown. Well, I'll just have to jimmy them open."

Unger pointed a threatening finger at Stark. "If you do, the estate will sue the police force. This is fine furniture, and since you have the keys, it isn't necessary to pry them open."

"All right." Stark looked at his watch. "Shit." He

called Ted Henry on his cell phone.

"What is it, Stark?" Henry whispered. 'Tm in the middle of a meeting."

"Did Anderton have keys on him?"

"Yeah."

"I'm going to send Harris to get them."

"Is that it?"

"Yeah."

Henry hung up.

Stark called Harris and told him to pick up the keys.

"Okay, Calvin, where's Bruce's bedroom?"

****

It took Harris an hour to get there.

"Where the hell were you?" Stark growled. "I've got to get over to Cranmer College."

"I was at the Hawley house."

"The Hawley House?"

"Nigel Hawley. Remember him?"

"What the hell were you doing there?"

"Patricia Hawley had a break-in."

"So, what the hell were you doing answering a B and E call?"

"Because nothing was stolen. That's why she called me. She had my card. Apparently her husband was paranoid about somebody breaking into the house, but he didn't want outside monitoring because the alarms are always going off by accident, she said. Anyway, he had a security company set up an internal system. It flashes a light in the master bedroom and there's a vibrator attached to the bed. Don't make a crude joke. There are little TV cameras in every room, and there's a monitor in the bedroom. When she got home last night, the light was flashing and the monitor was on. She played back the video, watched the intruder going through drawers, especially in her husband's office, looking through documents, not taking anything, putting everything back in place carefully. She saw the person leave the house, so she knew there was no danger. This morning she called me. I watched the video."

"Can you see who it is?"

Harris shook his head.

"Dressed like a Ninja, balaclava over his head, all in black, gloves, the whole thing."

"God. This thing is getting weirder by the minute. I don't suppose she had any idea what the guy could have been looking for?"

"The only thing she could think of is that her husband had a pretty valuable stamp collection, but he kept it in a safety-deposit box in a bank."

Stark shook his head.

"Okay. You have the keys?"

"Right here."

"I have to go over to the school, so I want you to look through Anderton's stuff, see whether you can find any connection with the other three, or anything, I guess, that might be a reason for somebody killing him. The guy was a forensic accountant—get the picture? Okay, I think it's this way, the kitchen. I'll introduce you to Calvin Unger, the butler from hell. What a miserable prick this guy is."

Chapter Nine

Diane Shapton made Stark feel good about himself. He would have said he had never fallen as hard quite so quickly, but that wouldn't have been true. Stark fell in love at the sound of a woman's laugh or the beam of her smile. He was staying home nights and reading instead of going to Carbo's: drinking two or three Scotches, not his usual six or seven or—since Carol Weems left—many more. He had to read like mad to have any chance in a discussion with Diane. She knew a hell of a lot more than he did. He no longer dreamed nightly of Weems. In fact, he wasn't aware of thinking about her at all, although he was. To Stark, everything had become Diane.

On the other hand, his feelings for her had not led to thoughts of this becoming a "relationship" a word he hated. Those thoughts hadn't occurred because he wouldn't let himself think such thoughts since Weems walked out. Powder the cat must have become confused because since Diane arrived, Stark had stopped saying to the cat—as he had every night since Weems had left, like an incantation—that a certain physical act was the only thing for which women were of any use. Perhaps that confusion might have been the reason Powder peed in the dieffenbachia pot, and not because Stark had forgotten to clean her litter box.

Shapton greeted him with polite formality, partly

because Kristin had escorted him into her office. But he could see there was more to it than that. She was tense. She looked her age.

"Will you need any more files, Ms Shapton?" Kristin asked.

"No, I don't think so. Thank you, Kristin."

The woman turned to go, hesitated, looked at Stark. For a moment, he thought she was going to say something. Her mouth opened, but she closed it quickly and hurried out of the room, shutting the door firmly behind her.

Shapton let out a deep sigh. Her hand was shaking.

"This seems to be affecting you more than the others did. Of course, Bruce Anderton went here more recently. I suppose you remember him, do you?"

She nodded.

"The school knows about this one?"

"He was a big contributor to the school, and, well, just generally well known in the city."

"Except by me."

"Well, he didn't move in your sort of circle. Oh, I'm sorry. It's just—"

"It's okay. I know what you mean. So, it looks as if somebody's trying to kill off all the graduates one by one. Don't look at me like that, Diane. I'm not being insensitive. We started with a connection among the first three victims and the mysterious Mr. Blaide, but they were here more than a decade before young Bruce Anderton attended the school. Blaide had been long gone, and so had the others. So, is there a link?"

She shook her head. "I don't know."

****

Calvin Unger was considerably more pleasant with

Noel Harris than he'd been with Stark. Perhaps he was impressed with Harris's politeness and consideration. Unger rapped on the door to Bruce Anderton's office. Harris was leafing through a file folder that he had removed from a stack on the right side of the desk to be deposited eventually on a stack on the left side.

"Would you like a coffee or tea, sir?"

"That would be very nice, thank you. Tea, please."

"Indian or Chinese, sir?"

"Oh, green tea would be nice, yes. Thank you."

"Most welcome, sir. Are you having any luck there?"

Harris sighed.

"He was very efficient. Makes it a bit easier. I don't understand the tables of numbers, but the reports are reasonably clear." Harris smiled and nodded at Unger.

"Yes, well, I'll get that tea."

****

Stark's first impression had been right. Shapton was more disturbed by Anderton's killing than she had been by the other three murders. He wondered whether his insensitive remark had hit a nerve.

The first killings had made some "sense," in that there were common elements. The only common element that was apparent in the latest killing at this point was the school itself. And if a connection to Cranmer were the killer's only motive, then the whole student body might be at risk.

Anderton's file shed no light, and Stark told Diane he would have to start interviewing the staff.

"That might not be the best thing," Shapton said with evident concern.

"You mean it will disturb the peace and good

government. Well, it will." There was a hint of exasperation in Stark's voice, his cop mentality and his impatience poking through the softness Shapton elicited. He heard the echo of his words in his head and tried to offset them with a smile. A knot tightened in his chest. Shapton's expression had gone hard. But it was a fleeting look. In an instant, her eyes twinkled again and she returned his smile, stood up slowly, coming around the desk, passing him, trailing her fingers along the side of his neck. She went to the door, locked it with an audible click, touched his neck again as she went by and sat on the edge of her desk, slowly crossing her legs.

"You don't have to do it right now, though, do you?" she said.

****

In the end, Harris carted all the files out to his car. Not only did Unger not protest, he even provided cardboard cartons.

Stark met Harris at Holtzman's.

"Well?"

Harris shook his head. "I can't see anything. Bruce Anderton nailed lots of people. It's full of court reports, that sort of thing. A lot of it are cases where the rules have been bent out of shape to make a company look better than it is. Some of it is fraud. There are a few heavies in there whose names you'd recognize. There's even a file on our old, no-longer-with-us pal Cataldi."

"What?"

"Yeah. Of course, he came out unscathed. 'No substantial evidence of fiscal wrongdoing,' it said. So, with your permission, I'm going to take the stuff to our fraud boys, and get them to have a look. They might spot something that an untrained eye like mine wouldn't see."

"Yeah, sure. They'll be delighted. You'll get a report on it in about a month."

"Not if Henry gets Peters to give them a push."

"All right. Now, tonight."

"Tonight?"

"Yeah, tomorrow it's hail, hail the gang's all here. I've got one night to see whether I can get anything on our buddy Blaide."

"But he couldn't have killed Anderton."

"Hey, remember that woman told you that you had to obey the Great One, or whatever they call him? Well, there you are. He doesn't have to do the killings. If it's part of the ritual, he'll have his minions do the dirty work. Probably earn them an indulgence, so they don't have to spend so long in purgatory before they're allowed into Hell."

"God. What have you got in mind?" Harris said in a pained voice.

"Relax. You don't have to do anything. Except go to the voodoo class."

"Jesus."

"I just want you to make sure that Blaide stays there."

"And then what?"

"And then nothing, if he is there. If he leaves, phone me. If I don't hear from you by seven-thirty, I'll know the coast is clear."

"What are you going to do?"

"What you don't know can't hurt you."

"Oh, yes, it can."

****

Stark listened to a Molly Johnson CD as he waited. When seven-thirty came, he gave Harris another seven minutes, and then he waited another minute and thirty-seven seconds to hear the end of a song.

The detective prided himself on his lock-picking skill, a talent he had acquired in a two-week course he had been given by Christopher "Quick Willy" Watson, in exchange for letting Quick Willy hide out in his apartment. Quick Willy was a skilful burglar, who had never been caught in the commission of a break-in. He had once been busted for possession of stolen property, for which he received an absolute discharge, since it was, technically, his first offence. He had been caught on that occasion only because his brother-in-law had turned him in. Stark liked Quick Willy because he never broke into residences, only businesses, and because he frequently provided Stark with information on violent criminals, offering information freely and without attaching conditions. Quick Willy got his name because of another, less-attractive habit of his. He had a compulsion to expose his dangling parts, but even in that, Stark found Willy amusing and considerate. He revealed himself only to matronly women, only in broad daylight, only on busy streets and only when there were at least two such women present. And never when children were in the vicinity.

"I wouldn't want to frighten anybody, Harry."

One might think that Willy's modus operandi would result in his being frequently apprehended. But in addition to his not wanting to inflict pain or suffering on anyone, Willy's choice of victim had another purpose.

"They get a kick out of it, Harry."

"They do?"

"Sure, I'm pretty well hung, you know."

"I'll take your word for it."

"They always laugh. Girlish giggles, I calls it."

Willy had been caught only twice, and years apart. Both times religion had played a role. On the first occasion, the two women were Jehovah's Witnesses out proselytizing. The second time, he pulled his stunt too near to a Catholic girls' school. "How was I to know they were nuns? They don't wear them uniforms any more. They just look like reg'lar women."

Stark hid Willy from the same brother-in-law who had turned him in—Willy's sister's husband, who was after Willy because he had taken money from the brother-in-law on the promise of leaving town, but had neglected to do so, instead losing the money in a crap game in Allan Gardens. In return for Stark's providing shelter, Willy had gifted him with a set of lock-picking tools, and showed him how to use them to open "any ordnery lock yer gonna find."

Stark switched off the CD and dashed across the road to Blaide's place. Blaide's flat was on the ground floor of a large three-storey house on the north side of Harbord Street that had been built for the owner of a shoe factory at the end of the nineteenth century. There was a wide veranda on the southwest corner of the building, and a deep entrance that kept Stark all but totally hidden from the street.

In less than a minute, he was inside.

"Whoa."

Stark staggered back as if he'd been shoved. If he'd had any doubt about whether he was in the right place, the array that confronted him dispelled that uncertainty in an instant. It was like an occult museum. Walls, tabletops, even the ceiling were festooned with ju-ju, charms and symbols. There were statuary of nymphs and sprites and faeries, incubi and succubi and Egyptian gods. There were brooms and bells and crystal balls, and knives with undulating, double-edged blades. Two scuffed ravens hung from the ceiling in a permanent swoop. The toothy mouths of African devil masks gaped menacingly.

It took Stark a moment to recover, and then he set about his task methodically, beginning at one corner of the main room and working his way along each wall, opening drawers, carefully removing their contents, examining them and returning them in the same order and position. Mostly, he found the kind of things encountered in the drawers of any house. There were copies of ordinary magazines, *Maclean's* and *National Geographic*. There were also more offbeat publications, including a stack of a weird monthly journal called *The World Beneath*. More ominous was a single copy of the *American Survivalist*, filled with ads for assault rifles and commando knives. The only object in the room that wasn't covered with supernatural icons was a baby grand piano. Stark lifted the lid, but there was nothing but piano works inside. Similarly, the kitchen cupboards and drawers contained nothing but dishes and food and culinary utensils.

As Stark was proceeding with his search, Noel Harris was frantically calling him on his cell phone, getting nothing but Stark's voice mail in response.

"What the hell is he doing?"

Harris had tried to leave the meeting room, but had been physically restrained by a very large man, who wouldn't let him leave until a certain part of some sort of cleansing ceremony had been passed. The Mage had been late entering, and when the door opened, it was not he who stepped into the room, but a much shorter, slighter person in a gold mask and blue gown, probably a woman. In answer to his urgent question, the fat woman had told him the Great One was taking the night off.

When Harris got to the parking lot, he found his car was blocked in. Stark's phone was not being answered because Stark had left it on the seat of his car when he went into Blaide's place. Harris ran out to Spadina and looked for a cab.

It wasn't until Stark found a photo album in the bookshelves in Blaide's bedroom-cum-den that he was able to say, "Aha." There were pages and pages of nubile nymphs and satyric-looking, bare-chested youths, draped in loincloths and white, diaphanous gowns, prancing in sylvan settings, like scenes from *Afternoon of a Faun*. Farther back in the book, the scenes began to get more raunchy. There was an artistic quality about what were clearly posed arrangements of now-naked bodies that lifted them above the level of porn, but it was unmistakable that they were meant to depict lust rather than idyllic love. Stark's real "Aha" came when he recognized that one of the youths, appropriately in a male embrace, was a teenaged Alan Sloane. He was easier to recognize because in adulthood, he had retained his boyish features. The other two, Chesley and Hawley, had grown older physiognomically. They could have been among the images in the book, but Stark couldn't tell. There was another book beside the photo album, filled with symbols and chants and spells and diagrams and instructions for rituals, including a detailed description on how to conduct a blood sacrifice with a chicken. Stark felt sick.

The rest of the search was fruitless. Stark had hoped to find some physical link to the crimes: notes about the victims' daily movements, for instance; even something with their names and addresses; newspapers and magazines with words clipped out that could have been used to write the Sweet Thursday notes; a daily journal or diary with incriminating notes; something before the details of the investigation got poured through the department sieve, before Blaide was alerted and destroyed the evidence. A computer in the room offered a ray of hope, but Stark's frustration was compounded when he found a password was required to get past the start-up.

"Shit."

He was hit with the need to urinate, and made his way to the bathroom. As he relieved himself, he slid open the medicine cabinet. Apart from an impressive supply of condoms and lubricant, there was nothing that he wouldn't have found among his own store of patent medicines, shaving tackle and deodorants. He slid the door closed, and heard as he did so the distinct click of a door opening, accompanied by the whoosh of car tires on the street. The floor creaked with slow steps, as if someone were moving cautiously, steps growing louder as they came nearer to his location, now too close for him to effect an escape, or find a hiding place. Stark was trapped.

He looked around. The shower curtain was closed. If the guy didn't want to engage in a complete routine of ablutions before retiring, Stark might be able to ride it out in the bathtub behind the curtain. The bathroom door was open. Stark could see shadows on the floor outside. He watched for one that was moving, reached behind him and pulled the shower curtain open as quietly as he could. The metal rings scraped on the curtain bar. He turned to step into the tub and involuntarily exclaimed: "Jesus."

The utterance was followed immediately by the sound of the footsteps hurrying toward him. He turned to face his adversary, reaching for his gun.

"It's me." It was Harris, nervously holding his hands in front of him.

"Jesus, Harris, why didn't you phone? Never mind, look at this."

Stark pulled the shower curtain fully open. Bathed in bloody water was the naked body of a man with a gold-handled knife protruding from his chest.

"Good God," Harris said. "It's Blaide."

They determined that the killing had occurred a short time before. They discovered that the rear door of the flat was closed, but unlocked. The attacker could have made his escape that way.

"Okay. Let's call the boys in."

"I hope your fingerprints aren't all over everything."

"Of course not," Stark said, holding up his hands, which were sheathed in surgical gloves. "I think I'm going to take something out to the car."

"What?"

"This family album. One of the pictures is of a young Alan Sloane. I don't think I'd better show it to you," Stark said archly. "The others may be in there, too, but I can't pick them out. And there's this other thing." He held up the black leather book. "It's got all kinds of sickening mumbo-jumbo in it, spells and chants and God knows what else."

"It's called a Book of Shadows."

"Book of Shadows." Stark shuddered. "You know something about this stuff?"

"I went to the library."

"Well, I don't want to let the Heavy Brigade in on anything more than I want them to know. I'll be right back."

Chapter Ten

The next morning, Stark rose at 6:45—like the middle of the night for him. Shapton was still asleep. Stark went to the front window and looked out on to Queen Street. The sun was shining, throwing long shadows. Traffic was crawling in both directions. The sidewalks had their own vehicular congestion: long lines of young mothers and nannies pushing strollers, interspersed with people walking dogs, every second one a golden retriever.

Stark went back into the bedroom and woke Shapton.

"Don't you have to go to work? School? Whatever you call it?"

"Mmm?" She looked at him through barely parted eyelids. "I'm going in late. One of the privileges of rank, and I'm not eager to tell them about the impending invasion by the boys in blue." She propped herself up on her elbow quickly. "When are you sending them in?"

Stark shook his head.

"Knowing would give me time to prep the principal."

"Sounds kinky."

"Down, boy."

****

The meeting at headquarters was scheduled for eight-thirty. Stark was to brief the troops. Wallace

Peters, the inspector nominally in charge of the Homicide Unit, would expect visual aids. Stark wasn't good at visual aids. He phoned Harris.

"You any good at visual aids?"

"What?"

"Listen, Peters will want one of those display things on the bulletin boards, a map with all the crime scenes circled, photos of each of the victims pinned beside the crime scene. A chronology—like that."

"Let me guess—"

"You don't have to guess. Get in there now and get working on it.

Harris sighed. "What time is it?"

"Six-forty-five."

"Six-forty-five? You've never been up this early in your life, and you sound like you're wide awake."

"Make it good. Peters thinks the case is solved if you have a nice display."

Diane Shapton was leaning against the doorway to the cluttered room Stark called his office. She was wearing Stark's shirt.

"Who's Peters?"

"He's the inspector who claims to run the squad, but most of the time he plays golf with the deputy chiefs, or engages in community relations. Ted Henry runs the unit."

Stark gave Shapton a kiss on the forehead as he hurried past her.

****

Harris had done a good job with the visual aids. Peters was impressed. He stood with his arms folded, studying the display, when Stark entered the room. Seeing him, Stark turned on his heel and tried to make his escape.

"Stark."

"Oh, yes, sir."

"Nice work."

"What?"

"On the display. Very good. Laying things out like this in a clear pattern is a tremendous help in investigations. I think I'm going to have some photographs of this taken for the address I'm giving to the Rexdale Rotary Club."

"Well, with all due respect, sir, I don't think that's a good idea. There's information there we wouldn't want the public to know."

"By then, we will, of course, have a solution to these crimes, won't we, Harry?"

"Of course, sir. Certainly."

Stark hated public speaking. He let Harris give the troops the rundown of events and answer most of the questions, popping up and interrupting only when he thought Harris was going to tell them something he didn't want them to know. Stark didn't like teamwork, but when he was forced to work with the whole unit, he made sure he ran the investigation, assigning well-disguised make-work projects to the klutzes, while using the competent officers as extensions of himself and retaining the essential part of the process. Teams were assigned to work with the Identification Unit and conduct tear-apart searches of the residences of everyone involved in the murders—victims and suspects alike.

After the briefing and a little practice for his Rotary Club appearance by Peters, Stark took Laurel and Hardy aside and told them that he didn't want to make a public announcement about it, but he thought there might be a homosexual ingredient in the killings, to which they both nodded in self-satisfied agreement. He assigned them to canvass the Gay Village and especially bathhouses and two gay churches, but he warned them to be extremely polite because Deputy Chief Bartek had already heard a complaint about the way they had behaved toward Alan Sloane's friend "and Bartek's son is as light on his feet as a ballet dancer on a bungie cord," which wasn't exactly rumour-mongering, because Deputy Chief Bartek had four daughters and no son. Stark assigned two other incompetents to check records of police forces throughout North America for crimes like these, and rank the cases according to similarities.

Marilyn, the unit's overweight and oversexed secretary, came up behind Stark, pressed her lips against his ear, making him pull away from her and turn his head, which she grasped and turned to face front again and returned her lips to his ear to whisper that he had a phone call, and then bit him on the earlobe.

"Jesus."

He took the call at his desk.

"Mr. Stark?"

"This is he."

"This is Kristin Montgomery, the secretary at Thomas Cranmer. I saw you in Ms. Shapton's office."

"What can I do for you, Miss—?"

"Mrs."

"Mrs. Montgomery. How can I help?"

"Well, I've been thinking about the three boys."

"The three boys?"

"Corbett and Nigel and Alan."

"Yes?"

The woman began sobbing. After a time, she said,

"Oh, my God, my God. It's a terrible thing. And now, oh God, young Bruce Anderton. There's something awful happening, Mr. Stark. Something awful. It's terrible, terrible."

"Yes, it is, Mrs. Montgomery. It's a very terrible thing, yes. But we're going to get the person who did this. We'll get him. Don't you worry now. And thank you for calling. Would you like me to send somebody to speak with you?"

"Speak to me? No—I, oh, it's so awful. Mr. Stark?"

"I'm still here."

"I thought I might be able to help."

"Oh, yes?"

"I knew them, you see. I've been here a long time at the school, and I knew all three boys. Well, I knew the Anderton boy, too, but he was very different. I didn't know him as well as I knew the others."

"You knew them. Well, I wonder—do you think you might have a look at some photographs, Mrs. Montgomery?"

"Photographs?"

"Yes. You might be able to help me out by looking at some pictures."

"Yes, well, if you think I could help. Of course I will, yes."

"Wonderful. I'll send a car for you. Where are you now?"

When the woman arrived, Stark took her into an interview room. He had the photo album from Blaide's apartment in a large manila envelope.

"Can I get you a coffee, Mrs. Montgomery? Or a soft drink?"

"No, thank you."

The little woman was nervous. Her eyes darted about the small room.

"Okay, well, just relax. I'm just going to show you a photo album."

"Is it one of those mug books you see on TV?"

"No, it's not."

Stark opened the book on the table in front of her. She looked anxiously from side to side, avoiding the album.

"Please, Mrs. Montgomery?"

She sighed and looked down. The pictures in the beginning pages were innocuous, all smiling youths demurely draped in white garments, like students at an innocent toga party organized by a prim spinster Latin teacher. Her fears quieted by this, Kristin looked up at Stark and smiled. She leafed through the book with approving nods at the tableaux of nice young people harmlessly enjoying themselves in a bucolic setting with nary a vodka cooler or a joint in sight. About a third of the way through, she stopped and looked up quickly at Stark with an expression of shock and scandal.

"Oh my gosh. It's Mr. Blaide."

"What? Where? Let me see."

There was a large photo centred on the page of a frontal view of a well-endowed, nude man holding aloft in a supplicating pose a long knife with a wavy blade, which Harris had told Stark was called an athame, a knife much like the one that Stark had seen pulled out of Blaide's chest at the autopsy. The figure in the photo was wearing a feathered, hawk-beak mask that covered his eyes, nose and forehead.

"How do you know it's Edward Blaide?" Stark asked uneasily, hoping he wasn't going to get an awkward answer.

She didn't answer, continued to look at the picture, and then her head jerked around to look at Stark.

"You know him?" she said. "You know Mr. Blaide?"

"I know who Blaide is, yes. How do you know it's he in the picture?"

"I know it's him by his beard."

The man had a sharply pointed goatee. When Stark had seen Blaide, he had no facial hair.

"Lots of people have little beards like that. How can you be sure it's him?"

"Because of the gap on the left side. He had a scar there, and the beard wouldn't grow over it. You can see the scar. Well, if you know it's a scar, you can make it out. The beard almost joins on that side, but not quite. When was this—oh, my God, what an awful picture—when was it taken?"

"I don't know. A long time ago, I suspect. Anyway, I'm glad you only recognize his beard."

"What? Oh, Mr. Stark, please—"

"I'm just kidding. I'm sorry. I shouldn't joke."

"No, this isn't funny. I want to turn the page."

The next few pages were relatively innocent, although Stark found their expressions increasingly suggestive. When she got to the photo of Alan Sloane and friend in a naked embrace, her hand went to her mouth and her shoulder slumped. Stark put a supportive arm on her shoulder.

"Are you all right? Can I get you a glass of water?"

"Oh my, oh my. This is terrible. This is awful. I can't look at this." She pushed the book away.

"I'm sorry, Mrs. Montgomery. I know it's very

distasteful, but it's extremely important in our investigation of the murders, you see. Do you recognize anyone in that picture?"

She looked at Stark and nodded.

"Who would that be?"

"I know both of them."

Stark looked at the photo. "You do?"

"Yes, the boy on the right is poor Alan Sloane. I'm not surprised that he'd be doing—that sort of thing. But the boy on the left—" She shook her head in dismay.

"The boy on the left? Who is he?"

"Peter Livingstone. Oh, God, his poor father."

"Peter Livingstone?" Stark looked at the picture again. "Who's Peter Livingstone?"

"Another student. What must his father have gone through? As if his death wasn't enough."

"His death?"

"Peter killed himself. He jumped off the Bloor Viaduct."

"God. When was that?"

"A long time ago. It was in all the papers. They couldn't keep it quiet. You must remember?"

"No, I'm afraid I don't. The papers don't usually write about suicides. Why did they cover this one?"

"Because of his father."

"Who was his father?"

"He was in the government, very high up."

"Wait a minute, Cameron Livingstone?"

"Yes."

"Yes. I remember now. Yes. He was—the minister of defence."

When the Montgomery woman failed to identify any of the other victims in the album, Stark prompted her, but she dismissed his suggestions as absurdities. Five minutes after he had given her into the hands of a constable to drive her home, Stark was smiling at his desktop, pleased that, after all these years, he was able to keep it pristine because he ran investigations in his own way, which meant that he was able to darken the doorway of the squad as little as possible. He was also amused because he kept it that way by shovelling things either into his desk drawers and filing cabinet, or into the wastebasket. The phone rang.

"Homicide, Detective Stark.—I'm sorry, what did you say?" He was racking his brain to remember who this was. The woman saved him from the embarrassment.

"Alan Sloane's sister."

"Yes, of course. Mrs. Kunservilus."

"Kuncevicius."

"Sorry. What can I do for you?"

"I was going through the guest room, and I found some stuff that Alan brought here a few years ago. It was in a big folder. He put it on the top shelf of a closet, behind a pillow, and he asked me not to touch it. I would never pry into his personal things, anyway. But he told me that it was there, because—" She sighed. "He knew that I'm a bit of a crazy-clean type, and he thought I would come across it. I never would have thought of it, except that a few months ago, he took it for a while and then brought it back. And I just remembered that today. Well, I opened it, and there's such an odd thing in it— Well, I don't know what it is, or whether it would help in your investigation. But his death is still so—I don't know. Incongruous is the word that comes to mind. And this is so strange that I thought—"

"What is it?"

"Well, it's a book, obviously quite an old book, a leather, ringed notebook, and it appears to have been my father's. I recognize the handwriting, and it's all in pen and ink. My father always used a proper ink pen. I say handwriting, but it's mostly printing and mostly numbers, groups of numbers. Perhaps you'd better look for yourself. There's also a key. It looks like the key to a locker."

"I'll be there in half an hour."

****

An hour and a half later, Stark was on the phone again, trying to calm down an irate Corinne Tremblay, the wife of the first murder victim, Corbett Chesley. She was furious that her privacy had been violated by a swarm of policemen. He finally placated her enough to ask her whether she had her husband's keys.

"I suppose so. Yes, I do. Why?"

"Do you know whether there's a key among them with the initials OYCCC stamped on it?"

"Just a minute." She put the phone down with a clatter that made Stark jerk the receiver away from his ear. Within the promised minute, she was back on the line. "Yes, it's here. It's his locker key from the Old York. I don't know why he still has it. He hadn't been a member there for years. God, it was before we were married. No, after that as well, because he used to come down for bonspiels from Ottawa."

"I'm going to send somebody over to pick up that key, Mrs.—Ms Tremblay."

"What for?"

"I'm sorry, I can't tell you. But it may well help find your husband's killer."

138

"It's like Corbett was the criminal instead of the victim. They're taking the place apart, prying into all our personal things. And this is the second time."

"The second time?"

"Yes. The police were here just after my husband was killed."

"Detectives Bradley and Pearce?"

"No. They were here on the day it happened, and then a couple of times after that to ask me questions, but they didn't search anything. No, two weeks after that, a policeman came. He was very nice, I have to admit. A real gentleman, perhaps because he was quite a bit older, but he wasn't a detective. He was in uniform. And he was extremely polite. He asked me would it be all right if he looked through my husband's papers just to see whether there was anything that might suggest a reason that somebody would want to kill Corbett, and I left him the spare keys and told him to put them through the mail slot when he left, and I went to work."

Chapter Eleven

"What do you think, Ernie?"

Noel Harris's boyfriend, Ernie Kowalski, a detective in the Intelligence Unit and also one of Stark's few personal friends, was leafing through the notebook Stark had given him.

"Yeah, it looks like code all right. We cracked a betting ring not long ago that had something similar. You want to know what it says?"

"Of course I do. Do you know anybody who might be able to decipher it?"

"Harry, you're out of touch. But, of course, I'm not saying anything that the world isn't aware of."

"What do you mean, I'm out of touch? Well, all right, I know what you mean. But why are you saying it about this code thing?"

"I mean because you're asking whether there's anybody who can crack it. Harry, it's a whole industry now, cryptography. And it's a big issue for law enforcement."

"There you go. That's why I'm out of touch about it."

"Well, many of the rest of us have been fighting against it, encryption, but it's a losing battle. Not only are all the corporations lined up against us, but also all the personal-privacy loons, all the civil-rights types. They teach this stuff in university now, Harry. There are whole university departments devoted to it. You're still not quite with me, are you? I'm talking about computers, Harry, the Internet. You follow?"

"I'm tuning in."

"Good. You know, we've always been able to tap a phone and gather evidence. But now even the mob is using the Internet to communicate. And that would be great, because that stuff's a breeze to monitor, but they're using encryption. It's all in code, and they change the codes on a regular basis. You have to have the key to figure out what's being said. It's a disaster for us. So, you want this decoded? Sure. It's a piece of cake. You see, we have to have our own encryption experts to try to crack the bad guys' codes. It's like espionage, for Pete's sake. We've even considered planting our own people in the encryption companies. You see, if we have the key, we don't care what the code is—we don't have to solve it. The key translates it for us. So, that's a long answer to your question. I'll get this thing turned into English for you in no time. What's this locker key?"

"It's another piece of the puzzle, Ernie. I told you the victims were connected through school. Now, it looks as if they might all have belonged to the same club."

****

Stark tossed the locker keys on the desk of Grant Sprocket, the club manager. Sprocket looked at the keys and then at Stark. He gave him a tepid smile.

"They're Old York locker keys. Where did you get them?"

"One belongs to Nigel Hawley, the other to a man called Corbett Chesley. Do you know him?"

Sprocket shook his head. "No, I can't say that I

know that name. I can look it up."

"No, that's okay. He used to be a member, a long time ago."

"Oh, well that explains it. I've only been here five years."

Stark resisted telling him he should have said he been there only five years. For some reason, he didn't like this man with a build like a narrow box, and he liked to correct the grammar of people he didn't like. But Carol Weems had told him it was boorish, and mostly he'd stopped doing it—except with Noel Harris and occasionally Ted Henry—just to annoy them.

"Tradition, eh?" Sprocket said, shaking his head appreciatively and holding up the keys as if he were venerating holy relics. "The design of these keys has never changed over the years. The lockers are still the same ones that were installed when the club was built seventy-three years ago. Actually, the club itself is much older than that, but—"

"Yeah, great. So, listen, there's another man who was a member, about the same time as this second man. I telephoned his sister before I came over here, and she confirmed he had been a member—Alan Sloane?"

"Alan Sloane."

"Yes."

"I don't recall an Alan Sloane, but there certainly was a George Sloane."

"George Sloane? This Alan Sloane's father was George, but he died more than five years ago."

"Oh, yes, I know that, but his name will live forever in the annals of the Old York."

"Good curler, was he?" Stark said, rolling his eyes.

"No-no, it wasn't that. He was a leading light in the

club. His name is on the trophy that goes to the club champion every year. There's also a five-thousand-dollar prize that's provided by a trust that Mr. Sloane established. He was very generous. Of course, the winner is expected to match the five thousand and make a donation to a worthwhile charity in the name of the club and himself and, of course, George Sloane. So, you say this Alan Sloane was his son. That could be. I don't know, but he's never been a member as long as I've been here, which is, as I say, five years."

"Is there anybody here—in the club today—who might have known Alan Sloane and Corbett Chesley?"

Sprocket toyed with the keys. "Let me think. Um— say, that's funny. That's quite odd."

"What's odd?"

"Well, two of these keys have no number on them. You see this one, it has the locker number stamped on it, 72. As I recall, that was poor Mr. Hawley's locker, but these other two, the one on the same chain as Mr. Hawley's and this other key, neither has a number on it. Oh, and, just a minute." He pressed the keys together and looked at them in the light from the desk lamp. "These keys are identical. That's very strange."

"Yeah, it is, because that key belongs to Corbett Chesley. What was he doing with exactly the same locker key as Nigel Hawley?"

Sprocket shrugged.

"Okay, look, let's go see which locker those keys belong to."

"My goodness, Mr. Stark, I'm not sure that—"

"You don't want me to get a warrant and send a team of policemen in here to stomp all over your locker room, do you?"

Sprocket sighed. "Very well, but it's going to take some time. There are five hundred and thirty-two lockers in that room."

"Yeah, well, maybe we'll get lucky. You take one key and start at one end, and I'll take one and start at the other. Let's go."

It took half an hour, with members coming and going and stopping to watch the two men trying the keys. When a member asked Sprocket what was going on, Stark interrupted him and said it was police business. Finally, Sprocket found the locker that the key opened.

"I've got it, Mr. Stark. Over here."

Stark looked at his watch.

"That's pretty good. Thirty-two minutes," he said as he walked down the ranks of lockers toward Sprocket's voice. "Whose locker is that?"

"Well, I don't know. I don't think we should open it."

Stark pondered a moment.

"No, in this case, you're probably right, not without a warrant. You don't know to whom it belongs?" Stark said, conscious as he carefully said it that the sentence made him sound like a pompous ass.

"No, but I can check the records."

In his office, Sprocket punched some keys on the computer.

"Locker three-twenty-seven belongs to Albert Baines."

"Who's he?"

"He's a minister, Mr. Stark."

"A minister? Minister of what?"

"An Anglican minister. His church is just down the road, on St. Clair."

"Well, we're still going to have to search it. I'm just

thinking, would you have a list of—who that locker has belonged to over the years?" Stark said, opting for less-pedantic construction.

"I'd have to get the old ledger books out of the vault, but the information would be in there. Do you want me to look?"

"Yeah, go ahead, get them out."

Sprocket gave a dry chuckle.

"Well, Mr. Stark, the only way I can find the names of all the members who have been assigned that locker is to go through years of ledger books and note down any time the locker assignment was changed. It's going to take a long time. In fact, I'm going to have to ask a couple of staff members to give me a hand."

Stark smiled wryly.

"But you're willing to do that if it obviates my having to obtain a warrant and going through the Reverend Baines's belongings."

"I don't know why you'd want to do that, anyway? What could the Reverend have to do with—any of this?"

"Who knows? So, are you going to check the books? If not, I can make a phone call and get the search warrant and leave you to explain to the parson why—"

Sprocket raised a hand.

"Never mind. I'll get started."

"How long do you think it will take you?"

"Several hours, I should imagine."

"All right. Here's my cell-phone number. Give me a call when you're finished. And hurry, because if you take too long—"

"I'll hurry, I'll hurry."

****

Stark waited for Harris at Holtzman's. He sat in the

145

private smoking booth at the back, with the door closed and the exhaust fan whirling and sucking out the smoke from his Gauloises. The thing was so powerful, it would lift a napkin off the table and devour it. Stark leaned too close to the fan and it started tugging at his shirt. He sat back, glowering with annoyance at the thing. It stared back dumbly.

"I'll fix you, you bastard," Stark said, switching the fan off and grinning sardonically at it.

In seconds, the door slid open.

"Turn the thing back on," Sid said with exasperation, "or stop smoking."

Stark sneered at Sid, and flipped the switch.

"Don't forget to tell me when Harris is here."

Holtzman shook his head and slid the door closed.

Stark took a deep breath. Sid's smoking booth was like an isolation box: it was good for meditating, thinking or sleeping—unless you had claustrophobia. Stark surrendered to the third possibility.

When Harris arrived, Sid had to shake Stark to wake him. He surprised the two men looking down at him by coming to life with a smile. In his slightly stuporous state, he was admiring Harris. Although he would never tell him so, Stark had begun to think of the good-looking young detective-constable as something like a son. He had dreamed about him, and although he couldn't remember anything of the dream, he knew it had told him that Harris was wasting his talent on the police force, because he had the potential to be a leader, and with his make-up, he would never rise beyond detective.

"Sit down."

Harris sniffed. "I'd rather not."

"Jesus. All right, we'll go sit at the counter."

Stark told Harris about the keys and the curling club and the book in code, and that Ernie Kowalski was getting the code deciphered.

"Why do you want to know all the people who used the locker?"

"Okay, listen…we've got five dead people all connected in at least one way—the school. Six, if you count Blaide, and you have to count him. He's a link, he's connected to all the dead people."

"Not to Bruce Anderton."

"Diane told me Anderton was involved in the same kind of mumbo-jumbo stuff the others were involved in."

"Who's Diane?"

Stark made a face.

"She's—Diane Shapton, the woman I've been dealing with at the school."

"And she told you that Anderton was into the occult?"

"Yes. So, it's entirely possible that he was part of Blaide's little group. So, six people connected through the school and maybe through Blaide. At least three of the group were also linked through the curling club—and not as members of the club. All three had keys to the same locker. I want to know who else was connected to that locker."

"Sounds like a wild-goose chase to me."

"It's not a wild-goose chase if Blaide's name comes up, or Anderton, or the Livingstone kid. You've got to tell me what happened with that, by the way, but wait till I finish. Okay, the locker's previous users may not help us at all. But it's just—let's just tie up all the loose ends."

"You know, none of this seems to be getting us any closer to the killer, or killers."

"It's got to be one person."

147

"Why?"

"All right, it doesn't have to be one person. I just think that it's one person."

"What about your theory of Blaide's followers doing the killings for him?"

"Yeah, that's Dia—Ms Shapton's idea, that they were all ritual murders committed on the order of Blaide—if not by him and that he then did himself in."

"You buy that?"

"At the moment, I don't buy anything. I suppose Blaide could have killed them because for some reason he thought the lid was going to blow and he was going to be connected to kiddie-diddling and black magic and what have you. But that doesn't—why after all these years? And then, after he got rid of all the people who could link him to the thing, then why kill himself?"

"What about the serial-killer thing? The month gaps, the Thursday business? Not to mention the athletic connection. What about all that?"

"I think that's a red herring. I think the guy wanted to make it look like it was a serial killer at work."

"Why would he do that?"

"Well, because all these people are connected. Whoever it was figured that if he just did them all in, we might start looking for a link among them, so he tried to provide us with a link, so we wouldn't look any deeper. That's what I think. If Henry hadn't given me the case, that might have happened. All that Sweet Thursday stuff."

"Why Thursday?"

"How the hell do I know? When we were kids, we used to say Thursday was fruit day. If you wore green on a Thursday, you were supposed to be a fruit."

"Very nice."

"Yeah, okay. We weren't the politically correct generation. I don't know why Thursday. Probably just to get us chasing the reason for Thursday. If Deputy Chief Whatsisname had been involved in the investigation, he'd have ordered fifty copies of Steinbeck's book and had everybody reading the thing to look for clues."

"Maybe that wouldn't be a bad idea."

"A stupid idea. Anyway, I did reread it," Stark said sheepishly.

"And?"

"You know, the trouble with that kind of approach is you can find a hundred possibilities if you look for them, none of them of any help in solving the bloody crime. I think he just picked Thursday to make it look more like a serial thing. So every Thursday that came around, we'd flood the streets with cops looking for joggers and swimmers and curlers and mountain climbers who might be the next victim. It was a red herring. My gut tells me that."

"What about this coded book? What's that got to do with anything? What do you think it is?"

"I have no idea, except Alan Sloane hid it. Look, it's probably nothing more than his father's diary. You know the way I do my investigations, Noel. No loose ends. I don't leave questions unanswered. I always want to know much more about a case than I need to know, because until I know everything, I don't know what I need to know. Get it?"

Harris made a gesture as if to say, "Whatever makes you happy."

"Hey, garcon, bring us each a cappuccino, will you, my good man," Stark said, smiling sweetly at Sid. "So," he said, turning to Harris, "what did you find out with

149

Cameron Livingstone's widow?"

Sid plunked two coffees in front of the policemen, slopping the black liquid on to the counter.

"It took some persuasion. She didn't want her son's name dragged through the mud. She didn't want the memory of her husband sullied. She didn't want the family to be in the centre ring of a media circus."

"Jesus. You can stop any time. I'm gagging. I hope you're quoting her directly."

"Anyway, it's probably just as well you sent me."

"You mean I would have been too brusque and insensitive?"

Harris made a face that said, "You're the one saying it."

"Okay, so what did she say?"

"I asked her whether her husband had been behaving strangely before or after her son had killed himself— 'tragically died,' I said, actually."

"Abusing the word 'tragically'. I've told you about that."

Harris ignored the remark. "I told her we had a suspect in her son's death. That made her leap. She said, 'What do you mean? He killed himself' I said 'Yes, of course, but we believe we know who was responsible for his suicide'. But I said we could advance faster on that if she told us more about her husband's behaviour. So finally, she admitted that 'he wasn't himself'.

"She said he was acting strangely. He started coming home later without calling her, and she said he always called to tell her he wasn't going to be home on time, and often would call two or three times during the evening. But about the time of the son's death, starting a couple of months before he died, he began the odd behaviour. She thought he was having an affair. I was surprised she said that. Anyway, something convinced her that he wasn't seeing anyone. She said he had an RCMP cop who drove him everywhere, but that he kept ordering the cop to drop him places and told him he'd take a cab home. The cop objected, of course, but I guess if the minister of defence tells you to get lost, what are you going to do? Then, just before he died, he resigned without warning. Just quit cold. He was dead within a week, massive heart attack. She said he had had a history of heart problems."

"What about the money? The bank account?"

"Oh, that hit a nerve. 'What business is it of yours,' she said. 'That's our private affair.' I had to run on the spot pretty sharpish there. Anyway, I had to tell her that we thought her husband might have been blackmailed about her son's activities. I could see she'd never thought of that before. It knocked the wind out of her. She got a lot softer, apologetic. She had to concede that she had nothing to do with finances, that her husband had handled everything. She said there were even bank accounts that she didn't discover till a couple of years after he died. But she said that at least she had kept all the books and all the bank statements, and she promised to get the accountant to look through them all, and see whether there were any large unexplained withdrawals about the relevant time."

"So, we're treading water. When did she say?"

"She said she'd take the stuff to the accountant tomorrow. Oh, there was something else. She said that on the day before he died, her husband locked himself in his office and she could hear the shredder going for hours."

Chapter Twelve

Christopher "Quick Willy" Watson stopped Stark on the street in front of Carbo's. Stark had arranged to meet Diane Shapton there for dinner.

"Harry, I've bin lookin' fer ya."

"What's up, Willy? No, wait. If it's that, I don't want to know about it."

"I'd a told you before this, only I was in the hoosegow."

"I thought you'd retired. Willy, you're too old for second-storey jobs now. God, you're too old for basement jobs. What did you do?"

"Naw, I'm all finished with that stuff, Harry. It wasn't that. It was, you know, the other thing."

"Ah, Jesus."

"I spotted these two nice lookin' young ladies on the street down by the waterworks."

"Young ladies? What, about sixty, were they?"

"They was a fine-lookin' pair, and old Willy started twichin'. So I did my thing. Quick-like, you know. The way I can do it."

"Quite a talent."

"Anyways, then I takes off, and the next thing you know, the cops is pickin' me up and throwin' me in the clink."

"But you're out already. Why didn't they hold you?"

"Because the two dears couldn't identify me is why.

See I've gotten smart, you know."

"No, I didn't know."

"Yeah, I put on one of them balyclavas so's you can't see my face, just my eyes, like. Works like a charm. Trouble is, I shouldn't do it around here, because the local boys in blue has got it in fer me. They always think I did it. When I works other parts of town, they never get me."

"Jesus, Willy, you can't go around in broad daylight with a ski mask over your face. They're going to think you're a robber. Somebody's going to shoot you, for heaven's sake."

"No-no, I doesn't go around wearin' it. I just puts it on quick-like, you know, right before I does my thing. And then I takes off and as soon as I gets around a corner, I pulls it off and shoves it down my pants."

"Yeah, nobody's going to look there. But surely when they got you to the lock-up, and you had to strip and shower, they found the thing, and that would probably be enough to nail you."

"I figured that, so I shook it down my pant leg when they put me against the wall for a frisk in the alley. Then when they took me to the car, I just walked away from it, clean as a whistle."

"So, is that what you wanted to tell me? Because I've got a date."

"No, that's not it. I wuz just tellin' you that so's you'd know why I hadn't told you before what I'm goin' to tell ya now."

"Okay, Willy, let's hear it." Stark looked anxiously at Carbo's door.

"I wuz in the alleyway behind your place, havin' a small snooze, you know, and I hears somebody goin' up your iron staircase there up to yer back door. Now, I know you never use that, and I know from experience that that's a route a thief's gonna take, so I get up from where I was restin', and I seen him."

"See who—whom?"

"Whom? No him. I seen him."

Stark sighed.

"Yeah, whom did you see, Willy?"

"The guy, the cop."

"You saw a cop?"

"Yeah, a uniform cop. He goes up the stairs and then he looks around to check he's alone. Then he does a real fast and fancy number on the lock. He's pretty good, this guy. He's in like he's got a key."

"A police officer? You're sure it was a police officer?"

"Hey, I guess I know a cop when I sees one, Harry."

"I guess you do. So you're saying a cop broke into my apartment, is that right?"

"That's what I'm sayin', yeah."

"Did you see him come out?"

"He was in there, I dunno, ten, fifteen minutes maybe."

"Did he have anything in his hands when he left?"

"Nuthin', and I wuz lookin' fer it, you know, watchin' close. He wuz barehanded."

"What did he look like? Could you identify him?"

"Maybe. He was thirty, forty feet away. But I can tell ya, he was an old cop, old guy. I mean, for a cop, he was an old guy, not a young cop, like most of them are, you know. He was older."

"Old for a cop. What, like forty?"

"Older."

"Older than forty. Was he driving? Was he in a scout car?"

"I didn't see no car. He walked down the alleyway and turned toward Queen Street. That was the last I saw him." Willy shrugged.

"Hmm. Well, thanks, Willy. Here, get yourself a hamburger."

Stark slipped a twenty-dollar bill into the old man's hand.

"Who needs a security guard when you've got Quick Willy watching out for you, eh?"

"Thanks, Harry. Yer a gent."

When Stark finally entered Carbo's, he saw Diane Shapton sitting in the front corner, near the window. She looked tired. Even though she was older than Stark, he never thought of her that way. Tonight, she looked as if she was in his decade. In fact, another observer would have put her down as older than he, but Stark wouldn't allow himself to see her like that.

The years of *In Praise of Older Women* had longed passed for Stark. He kissed her on the cheek.

"Why didn't you sit at the back, in the smoking section? We could have had a cigarette."

"They won't let you smoke your Gauloises in here, Harry. You know that."

"I bought some Player's especially for the occasion."

"Never mind, we'll smoke after. We always do." She smiled coyly and suddenly looked like a little girl. "So, how's the case going?"

"Oh, it's moving along."

"Oh yes?"

"I shouldn't tell you this, but just to put a little spice

in the evening: there's a book in code."

"A what?"

"A book in a secret code. Now, that's all I'm going to tell you. But how about that? Mysterious stuff, eh?"

"Very."

"Oh, and this is really weird. This has nothing to do with the investigation, so I can tell you this. Some cop broke into my apartment."

"What?"

"Yeah. Remember I told you about Quick Willy Watson?"

"The flasher."

"Yeah. Well old Willy is harmless." Stark leaned toward her. "His old Willy is harmless."

"I'm glad it's not catching."

"Not a chance. Anyway, Old Willy keeps out of sight mostly. He often sleeps behind an old car Jimmy Yu keeps threatening to restore. It's on blocks in the lane behind my place. Willy's got a big cardboard box and newspapers crushed down into a bed, and I gave him a heavy plastic drop sheet, and I bought him this super-insulated sleeping bag. He prizes that thing, has it strapped to his back from October to May. I store it for him for the summer. If it's really cold, I let him come in and sleep in that little storage room I have in the back."

"You're a nice man, Harry, even though you pretend not to be."

"Hey, don't tell anybody. So, anyway, Willy was taking a siesta in the lane the other day and he heard a guy going up my back stairs. He looked and saw it was a cop in uniform, and the guy went to my back door, and used a pick to open it, and went inside. Willy used to be a burglar, so he admired the guy's work."

"When was this?"

"Three days ago. I didn't notice anything. The guy wasn't there to steal anything, or if he was, he didn't find anything. He was an older guy, too, which is a bit surprising, although maybe not. I don't know. I'll have to get an internal investigation started tomorrow. I have no idea what the heck he was doing there. It's quite bizarre. Hey, if you can't trust a cop, who can you trust, eh? I'll tell you something for nothing, my dear, I'm one cop you can't trust. Trust me on that. So, did the heavy mob move in to the school today?"

"The heavy mob? Oh, you mean the police. Yes, they were there. They phoned the principal before they came, and he called an emergency meeting of the staff and told them to keep their mouths shut, that they weren't to lie, of course, but they weren't to volunteer information. No 'mouth-flapping,' was how the bugger put it. They're scared to death that this is going to blow their reputation all to hell. You said you'd send Harris. You let me down, Harry."

"Sorry. I had to give him another detail."

"Anyway, it was fine. They interviewed a few of the older staff members, looked through the files of the four who were killed, photocopied them, and left. Afterward, the principal called another meeting, and wanted to know 'precisely' what the staffers had told the police. He was clearly relieved, because they didn't know anything to tell them. And you told me not to tell them anything about Blaide, so I didn't."

"That's good. I'll tell them about Blaide—when I think they need to know it."

****

"I told you we'd smoke afterward."

"A little bit during, a couple of times there, I think."

"Oh, you're hot stuff all right, Harry."

"'Hot Stuff Harry'. I like that."

"You would. So, come on, tell me about this coded book. Maybe it's Blaide's magic spells and that sort of thing."

"I'll tell you this, it's nothing to do with Blaide's spells. And that's all I'm going to say on the subject. You want a drink, or a coffee or something?"

"No, I'm too tired. You tired me out, Hot Stuff. I think I'll just go to sleep. So, are you going to be able to crack this code?"

"Diane."

"Well, that's not telling me anything, for heaven's sake."

"Okay. Last comment on the subject. After this, my lips are hermetically sealed."

"Oh, I hope not."

"The answer is, yes. We have a code expert working on it right now."

Shapton kissed him on the cheek, said goodnight, and rolled over.

When he awoke, she had already left. There was a note on the kitchen table explaining that she wanted to go to her place to wash her hair before she went to work.

At nine o'clock, the phone rang. It was Ernie Kowalski.

"It's going to take a little longer."

"Why, is it a tough code?"

"No, that wasn't the problem."

"Wasn't the problem?"

"Right, wasn't. We finally solved it. In fact, I solved it."

"Hidden talents."

"Lucky guess. The guy ran it through every sort of program he had. It just kept coming back gibberish. Finally, it dawned on me. I said, 'You're trying to change this thing into English, right?' The guy got mad. He said, 'Isn't that the idea?' I said, 'Well, what if it's not in English?' He said, 'Then we've got a real problem, because unless you know what language it is in, I'm going nowhere.' I said, 'What if it's in Russian?'"

"Why Russian?"

"Why not? Secret code, the timing would be right, Cold War."

"Cold War? Come on, Ernie, this thing isn't—"

"Hang on. Just wait. So the guy said, 'I'm still screwed, because I don't know Russian, and I haven't got a program for Russian.' 'Okay,' I said, 'have we got somebody who can do Russian?'"

"Can you cut to the chase?"

"Okay. The guy did know somebody—in Ottawa, so we scanned in the book. There are only sixteen pages that were written on. We sent it to the guy in Ottawa by the Internet. And two hours later, he's got it cracked and translated."

"It was in Russian?"

"Yep."

"Jesus. What the hell's going on here? And you say the guy did that in two hours? Translated it from Russian to English?"

"No, that's why I said we're going to be a little longer, like not till tomorrow. I'm going to translate it into English."

"You?"

"What's my name?"

"Kowalski. That's not Russian. You're Polish."

"How old am I, Harry?"

"What's that got to do with anything?"

"Because I didn't come to this country until I was fifteen. And when I was a kid in Cracow, we had to learn Russian. And believe me, speaking Russian in the crime-solving biz in this day and age is a very useful thing."

"Okay, so we're stuck till tomorrow. Any idea what time?"

"Take it easy. You'll get it as soon as I can get it done. I'm supposed to be working on a bike-gang thing."

"As soon as you can, please—and thanks."

Stark hung up the phone, and his cell phone rang in the bedroom. He didn't hear it over the kettle whistling, and just got there on the fifth ring, in time to beat the voice mail. It was Grant Sprocket from the Old York.

"I've got the information you requested, Mr. Stark."

"And?"

"That's all you wanted, wasn't it? Was there something else?"

"I meant, and what did you find out? Whose locker was it? I'd better get a pen."

"I don't think you'll need a pen."

"I won't?"

"The only two members who have used that locker in the past half-century were Albert Baines, who has it now, and George Sloane."

****

"Nice of you to show up, Stark," Detective Bernie Bryden said. He was sitting in the Homicide squad room, playing cribbage with his partner, John Hardy. Two other detectives were typing notes. "Got any more fag patrols you want to send us on? Christ, you're supposed to be running this investigation, and where the hell are you? Nobody knows, for fuck sake. Jesus."

"Harry—" Ted Henry stuck his head out of his office. "—I want to see you now."

Bryden and Hardy gave Stark mocking looks. He stared back at them blankly. Henry was holding the door open for him. He shut it behind him loudly. "Stark, you could get a reprimand for this."

"For what?"

"For what? For nothing, that's what. Jesus Christ, Bryden's right. How many times am I going to have to say this? It's a team effort, for God's sake. You get it? Team? These guys have been in here all morning. And yesterday, you're sending in instructions with Harris. He doesn't rank with these guys. It's insulting to them, and they're not going to do what he tells them."

"I've been busy. I'm working on four murders."

"What the hell do you think these guys are supposed to be doing?"

"Don't blow a gasket."

Henry took a deep breath and held it until he felt controlled enough to release it. As calmly as he could manage, he said, "Peters wants a written report. Now. Not later today. Now. Do it now. And where are you in this thing? Tell me, for God's sake."

After Stark finished giving Henry what he made sound like a complete account of what he had been doing and what he had discovered, but leaving out many of the key ingredients and emphasizing and embellishing the inconsequential, he emerged from the office, promising to type a report. He closed Henry's door, so he couldn't hear him tell the four detectives that the detective-sergeant wanted them to go to the Old York and interview everybody in sight, because somebody must have seen something.

"Christ, it's a bit late now, isn't it?" Bryden said.

****

The Star had an enormous file on George Sloane, all of it on microfilm. Stark took notes. Sloane was too good to have been true, a credit to capitalism, a paradigm of philanthropy, eminently successful in business, the details of which were rarely mentioned. There were one or two articles that had appeared in the business section about the several companies he operated, all of which seemed to be international in character, involved in shipping and trade. He was credited with providing seed money to the new ventures of hopeful young men with grand ideas. Most of the pieces were about his generosity to various charities, especially aid organizations working with the less-fortunate citizens of the world's poorer regions. His name graced a number of sports trophies, for which the city's finest physical specimens still competed in various forms of athletic endeavour, but it was the development of the mind that he preferred to encourage, establishing many trust funds to provide scholarships and bursaries in several academic disciplines.

That Stark had never heard of him before, despite his considerable benevolence, was explained by several references to Sloane's eschewing the limelight, refusing to pose for photographs and never granting interviews, the allusions to which were given with admiration, not the resentful tones journalists usually use when they are frustrated in their pursuit of a quarry. The first mention of Sloane was in 1947, when, at the age of twenty-nine, he had won a curling bonspiel at the Old York Cricket,

Croquet and Curling Club. Even at that young age, he was described as a successful businessman, "a rising star in the firmament of commerce." There was never a reference to his origins, or his education. He was identified either as a Torontonian or a Toronto native, and more than once as a great Canadian. There was no indication of military service, although his age was such that, as a "great Canadian," he would have been expected to have fought for his country against the Nazi tyranny, but perhaps that was explained by a few photographs showing him with a cane.

Harris was waiting for Stark in the cafe of the Loblaws store on Queens Quay. He was eating a sandwich, and there were two shopping bags at his feet.

"That's why you wanted to meet me here," Stark said, indicating the bags. "Let me guess, stinky cheese and brie, three or four kinds of hummus, two kinds of olives and an assortment of ethnic foods. Have I got it?"

"Try Froot Loops and Kraft Dinner."

"Oh, gourmet stuff. What's this?" Stark held up a cereal box. "Super High Fibre, made with the floor scratchings from an Albanian stable, no doubt."

"That's for Ernie."

"A bit irregular is he? No, you don't have to answer that. I know the answer."

"Cut it out. It's not becoming."

"You're right. I'm sorry, Noel. I shouldn't make remarks like that. I'm just a coarse and vulgar swine and I can't help myself. The truth is, I'm glad you and Ernie are still together. You're good for each other. You're a nice couple. God, what did I just say?"

Harris laughed.

Stark smiled warmly, looked at the young detective

for a moment and then gave his head a little shake to get it back to the matter at hand. "So what did you find out from Mrs. Whatsername?"

"Livingstone. Nothing new," Harris said, wiping his lips with a paper napkin.

"Nothing? No unexplained cash withdrawals? No odd movement of money?"

"Nope. Her accountant said that Cameron Livingstone kept scrupulous records, and that he, the accountant, handled most of the transactions. A lot of the stuff was held in blind trusts because Livingstone was in the government. Livingstone withdrew a regular allowance that never varied until the day he died. There's no indication that he was paying off any blackmailer."

"Let me tell you what I've been finding out—"

Chapter Thirteen

Diane Shapton told Stark she had work to do that evening, so he set out for Carbo's. Halfway there, he changed his mind, bought a burger and fries in Lick's and took them home, where he read Charlotte Bronte's *Villette* for an hour, absently stroking Powder, who was pleased to find him home alone, and had decided to take advantage of it with a session of forehead-rubbing and hand licking. When Stark had had enough of Lucy Snowe, he put the book down, switched on the TV and watched the hockey game: the Leafs and the hated Philadelphia Flyers, a team he had detested since the days of the Broad Street Bullies. He felt good when the Leafs surprised him and won. He switched off the television and prepared for bed. During the course of the evening, he had smoked a pack of Gauloises, but had drunk only two beers. He was oblivious to both facts. The phone rang.

"Yeah?"

"Is that how you usually answer the phone?" It was Ernie Kowalski.

"That's not how I usually answer the phone, but it is how I answer the phone at this time of night."

"It's ten-fifteen," for Pete's sake.

"Hey, does this call mean what I hope it means?"

"All translated, and it's going to blow your socks off I'm coming over."

Kowalski declined a drink, and Stark made a pot of coffee.

"You want a doughnut or something? Not that I have any, but I might have some cookies."

"I don't want anything. Do you know what this is?" Kowalski held up a thick wad of paper, on which handwriting was visible.

"What?"

"Among other things, it's a set of instructions, procedures, that sort of thing, for a secret agent of the government of the Union of Soviet Socialist Republics."

"Ah Jesus. Come on."

"Have a look for yourself. Unless this is the most complicated and bizarre joke I've ever heard of, these are the notations of a Russian spy."

"What?" Stark took the sheaf of papers and began leafing through them. "What do you think these locations are about? 'Fifth brick from the ground, behind the organ pipe cactus in the westernmost greenhouse in Allan Gardens.' And here's a reference to a loose grave marker in St. James Cemetery."

"Well, what do you think they are?"

Stark shrugged.

"Document drops?"

"Exactly."

"God." Stark shook his head. "Here's some phone numbers. This is an old book. Look, this one's Gladstone 2473. These three are more recent, Ottawa numbers, all 613s, initials beside them CC, AS and NH. Jesus. Corbett Chesley, Alan Sloane and Nigel Hawley. Holy shit."

"And they are?"

"They're three of the murder victims."

"The ones that went to school together?"

"There was a fourth one. He went to the same school, but years later."

"So why would their initials be in a Soviet spy's notebook?"

Stark shook his head.

"I am truly impressed, Ernie." Stark held up the papers. "This is remarkable. I thought you Polacks were supposed to be stupid."

"Hey, listen, Kowalski means genius in Polish."

"You're kidding?"

"Yeah, I'm kidding. Kowalski is one of the most common Polish surnames. It's a derivative of the word kowal, which means blacksmith."

"Is that right? Well, you're one smart blacksmith, my man. Now, let me tell you about the guy this book is supposed to have belonged to. On the other hand, from what I know about this guy, and what I'm going to tell you, I think you'll agree, this whole thing sounds awfully unlikely—"

They agreed that the book should go to CSIS eventually. They also agreed that asking CSIS for help would be a waste of time.

"If this guy Sloane was a spy, I might be able to help you out," Kowalski said.

"Oh, yeah?"

"Well, because of the various activities of some of our recent immigrants, I now find myself in frequent contact with my opposite numbers in the Russian police, where my ability to speak the language has proven invaluable, not only because it makes communication easier, but also because they tend to trust me more. I tell them I'm Ukrainian. There's one chap I've got to know quite well, who used to be in the KGB. He's never actually said so, but from what he has said, and what I know about the times he's talking about, I know he was KGB. A lot of their old files are open. And they've been giving selected, i.e. fairly useless, information to the West. I wouldn't be surprised if CSIS already has the file on this guy—if he was a spook—but they're not going to tell us. Anyway, let me ask. He might be able to get the information for us."

"Jeez, I'm just remembering that she said the book was in his handwriting."

"Who? She who? Whose handwriting?"

"The daughter of this Sloane guy. She's also the sister of Alan Sloane—one of the victims."

"Right."

"And she said the book was in her father's handwriting, so, bizarre as it seems, it looks as if Mr. Wonderful, the great Canadian, was a Russian spy. My God."

"Okay, well, I'll give it a shot. Now, I'm going home. I'll call you tomorrow early, because those guys are eight hours ahead of us. In fact, as soon as I get home, I'll send this guy an email. By the time I get up tomorrow, I may have the information."

****

Stark put Noel Harris in charge of determining who the phone numbers had belonged to.

"You'll have to get Bell to research the really old ones. Those Ottawa ones are government departments. I checked that this morning. I'm going to go over and roust the Reverend Baines. I think he might be the ringleader."

"What are you really going to do?"

"I'm not going to do anything. I'm waiting for Ernie to call. I don't want to tie up the phone."

"Why don't you get call waiting?"

"What, so I can put one telemarketer on hold, while I answer the call from another one? Anyway, I think I do have it. It came with the package. I wanted the call display thingy, so I could see when Ted Henry was calling."

"And I imagine he has been. He was steaming mad because you didn't do the report for Peters."

"The hell with Peters. Anyway, I headed that one off at the pass."

"How?"

"I called last night, when I knew that Ted wouldn't be there, and left a message on his phone saying I hoped that Inspector Peters found the report that I left on his desk to be as detailed as he required."

Harris shook his head.

"I don't believe it."

"Henry won't believe it either, but it'll get him off the hook. I also gave him a more complete report this time on what we've found."

"Which seems to be sending us off in every direction, but I don't think we're getting any closer to the killer. Do you?"

"Just relax, Noel. I'm feeling good."

"You're not on Prozac or something, are you?"

"No, I'm not on Prozac."

"Ah, the snarl. That's more like it."

"Just find out about those damned numbers, all right?"

Stark ushered Harris to the door, gave him a light shove through it, and closed it quickly behind him. The phone rang. Thinking it was Kowalski, Stark ran and answered it without looking at the call display. It was

Ted Henry.

"Stark, what the hell are you doing?"

At the end of a long interchange that waxed and waned in intensity and volume, Henry had vented his anger sufficiently to emit a small chuckle. "Now, I'm not just calling about that business, I've got some useful information. At least, it may be useful."

"What's that?"

"The lab boys finally decided to take the bits of paper that were used to write the Sweet Thursday notes off the, you know, the sheets of paper they were stuck to. Are you following this?"

"Sure," Stark said, shrugging because he didn't know what Henry was talking about.

"Okay, so they look on the back of the bits of paper, and there's enough stuff on two of the pieces for them to figure out that they were clipped from one of those suburban giveaway papers."

"So?"

"So, it's a North Toronto paper, actually it's what used to be North York."

"Oh, that's very helpful, Ted."

"Take it easy. Just wait. I wanted to find out what issue it was, what day it was printed. I thought it might help, who knows. So, I sent somebody over there, and we got lucky."

"How's that?"

"It turns out there's a serious error on one of the pieces of paper. They got the name wrong of somebody who's a big advertiser, and they spotted it just after the presses started running, so they were able to stop the presses and correct it, but one truck got out. Anyway, they called the guy back, and when he got back, there was a bundle missing. Anyway, it turns out the delivery kid picked up the bundle right away and delivered all the papers. So they just said forget it. Anyway, this is one of those papers. So we know exactly what neighbourhood it was delivered in."

As soon as Stark hung up the phone, it rang again. This time it was Kowalski.

"Harry, we hit the jackpot. I'll be there in fifteen minutes."

"The guy faxed me the whole file. It's sort of semi-declassified." He handed Stark eight letter-size sheets of paper stapled together.

"What's that supposed to mean, semi-declassified?"

"It means, it's not really supposed to be released, but there's nothing embarrassing in it for the current government, so it's easy for somebody like my contact Yuri, who, I told you, used to be a KGB guy—it's easy for him to get at. It's no skin off his nose, and he's paid back a favour to me, and now I owe him one. That's the way it goes."

"So, what's it say? In case you didn't notice, Ernie, it's in Russian."

"Oh, yeah, right. Sorry. Okay, you'd better make us a pot of coffee—"

Kowalski's translation was smooth and practically seamless. As he had been many times in his long friendship with this awkward looking giant of a man who seemed coarse and obtuse, Stark was once again impressed with Ernie's knowledge and ability.

"It starts with a lot of clerical details, ID number and so on. He was born in Saransk in 1918. His name was Aleksei Slobodin, graduated from Kolonma Military Academy in 1934, Moscow State University in 1939.

Obviously a brilliant student, because he obtained a masters in economics at the age of twenty-one? Trained 1940 at the Moscow Language Institute and with the GRU in Minsk, posted to Ottawa in 1941. He would have been twenty-three. Worked officially as an attaché to the Soviet ambassador, but was actually a GRU officer with the military rank of lieutenant. Promoted to major—in six months. My God, he must have done good work. Took extension courses in English and French at the University of Ottawa. God, we're helpful to foreign spies, aren't we? He became George Sloane in 1943.This is interesting. Details how he did it. Nothing new here, but it always amazes me that it works so well and so easily. He found the name of a child who had died in his first year of life by examining grave markers. Got the name of the parents from newspaper records of the obituary notice. Applied for a birth certificate, which was granted. Used that to get a passport, driving licence, other identification. He was now George Sloane, aged twenty-five.

"Now, let's see. Okay, it doesn't explain this, but somehow he's suddenly operating and owning an export/import business, Vanguard Optical Equipment in Toronto. They liked their little jokes. Vanguard?"

"The workers' vanguard, I get it."

"Joined the Toronto Rotary Club. That's amusing. Ah, here's where he began his sporting life. Joined the Old York Cricket, Croquet and Curling Club in 1945. He would have to have been sponsored.

"Probably, he would have made contacts in the Rotary Club. Of course. It mentions his skill as a curler. I'm not surprised. I know the way they work. Or did in those days. He would have read every book on the subject he could find, he would have done all the recommended exercises, and they would have found somebody, probably some old Uke socialist from Saskatchewan, to train him.

"They'd have trained him in business the same way. And he would have been so indoctrinated, so committed to the cause, that he'd work at it eagerly, no leisure time, constant learning, training, practice, five hours' sleep a night. They had to prove their system was the best, and it was—if you wanted to turn people into perfect machines. He wouldn't have done anything that didn't help the mission in some way."

"More coffee?"

"Yeah, thanks. So, after that, it's mostly about building up his business holdings, buying a film-processing company and an electronics wholesale business. Very useful acquisitions for a spy. Ah, here we are. He makes contact with agent 5324X-A, whoever that is. And then there's a bunch of stuff about building relationships in the business community, oh, and the political community. Establishing a deep cover. He seems to be doing that very well. He joins the Liberal Party in 1949.What else? Here we are, vice-president of the Toronto Board of Trade in 1950. Member of the Heritage Society, on the board of the Red Feather campaign, vice-chairman of the Society for Crippled Civilians, more stuff like that. Yeah, he really was going deep. Donations of money to the University of Toronto, the Crippled Civilians, Red Cross and so on. Nothing about any espionage activities. But, of course, he'd be doing things all along. There'd be three main purposes for a guy like this.

"First of all, he'd give tiny pushes, policy pushes in

the desired direction, either toward something that would be helpful to something they wanted helped, or even the opposite, like hardening attitudes. Nothing better for communism than the polarization of the bourgeoisie and the proletariat. And then he would have been an incredibly disruptive influence because he'd be able to sow little seeds of discontent. Turn one group against another with a word or two in the right ears.

"And third, especially with his contact in the Liberal Party, he'd be able to inform his masters about the direction of the economy, about planned investments, about things like overseas contracts that Canadian companies were bidding on. He'd also know who was vulnerable, who was going broke, who was gay. He wouldn't go after them. That wouldn't be his role, too risky. Other operatives would make an approach.

"Jesus. Here he gets married, 1956, Annabelle Bonham. Little bit about her, born in Ancaster, Ontario, in 1932, quite a bit younger. He was thirty-eight; she was twenty-four, educated at St. Hilda's Academy and, oh boy, Harvard. Degree in Political Science. Of course. Ah, here's where they got her. Spent a year at the London School of Economics. Oh right, three months as an exchange student at Moscow U. Yeah, right. Finally, in 1972, he's establishing a small cell, four members, not including him. See, here's that agent 5324X-A again. I get the impression that this agent with the number is the only contact Sloane has with the cell. That's about it. There's some stuff about commendations. Jeez. He was given the Order of Lenin. They must have been happy with him."

"That's all? Nothing about what this cell did, or who was in it, or anything like that?"

"No. What there are are a bunch of cross reference numbers to other files. One's a correspondence file, for instance. I imagine that all the details of their activities would be in the other files. I don't think I'd have any joy asking my guy for these, though. I can try."

"Yeah, you may as well."

"So, how does this advance your murder inquiry?"

"I just don't know. When you said we'd hit the jackpot, I thought this was going to have all the answers."

****

After Kowalski left, Stark wrote his report for Peters. He headed it Summary of Findings, and, in point form, produced a series of vague notes, finishing with one that said an arrest was imminent. When he got to headquarters, he grabbed a sheaf of circulars, and stapled the "summary" to them. Peters would be delighted to find he didn't have to read beyond the first page.

Fifteen of the members of Edward Blaide's Magic Circle had been located and interviewed. None had provided any useful information. Detectives Ray Bradley and Bill Pearce encountered Stark in the squad room.

"Harry, you may want to sit in on this one," Bradley said.

"What one?"

"One of the members of the coven, or whatever the hell it is, has come in voluntarily. We're tracking down all the others. They've all made themselves scarce. This woman's petrified."

"Let's go."

A fat woman sat at the table in the interview room, staring straight ahead, her hands together on the table in front of her, fingers interlaced. She had a face in which none of the features seemed properly lined up, as if somebody had given it a twist.

Pearce switched on the tape recorder.

"Ms Pender, this is Detective Harry Stark. He's in charge of the investigation," Bradley told the woman and the tape recorder. "My name is Detective Ray Bradley, and with me is also Detective Bill Pearce. This is Madeleine Pender," he informed Stark. "She has something to tell us about the death of Edward Blaide."

"Not his death," the woman said quickly, her head moving for the first time. Only one side of her mouth moved, and she spoke in a girlish voice. "I don't know anything about that."

"Whatever it is you have to tell us," Bradley said, smiling solicitously.

"You were in the group that Edward Blaide ran, is that right?" Stark said.

"I still am." She held her head high. "No one runs the Magic Circle. The Mage was our guide, not our controller."

"We've been told that anyone in the group would do anything the Mage asked him or her to do. Is that not correct, then?"

"We would do anything that the Great One asked because he is our guide from the Other, and we would not question his wisdom, but we would be free not to obey if we so chose."

"So, in a nutshell, you would all pretty well do whatever Blaide asked."

She raised and turned one hand as if to say, "Probably".

"Okay, Madeleine, what else do you have to tell

us?"

The woman's head turned quickly toward Stark, and then jerkily, to stare suspiciously at Pearce and Bradley in turn. She faced front again. The mobile corner of her lip quivered slightly. There was a hitch in her breath. She said nothing.

Stark and the other two detectives exchanged glances. Stark began to say something at the same time as Pender started to speak. They both stopped. She let her breath out audibly.

"The Mage was frightened," she said. "We all knew he was frightened."

The detectives looked at each other again.

"How did you know he was frightened?" Stark asked.

"We heard him. We were leaving the gathering, and we heard him talking on his cell phone in the preparation room."

When she stopped for a while, Stark asked, "What was he saying? Could you hear?"

"He said, 'You promised me no more. After all these years, why?' And then he said, 'They think I did it. They know, they know, they know.' He kept saying it. And then he said, 'They're going to get me. I know it.'"

She stopped again. After a time, Stark said, "Was that it? Did he say anything else?"

"He said, 'You know him? What do you mean, you know him?' And then he said, 'I'm frightened.' And then he said, 'Of course I should be frightened.'" Pender took a deep, gulping breath and her shoulders slumped. It was clear she was finished.

"Do you know who he was talking to?" Pearce said.
Pender shook her head.

"The witness is shaking her head," Bradley said. "I take it that means no?"

She nodded.

"Do you mind speaking—for the tape."

"I don't know who it was," she said.

Stark said, "You don't know who it was, but do you have an idea who it might have been?"

"No."

"Was Blaide, or any member of the group, ever threatened, do you know?"

"No."

"No, no one was threatened, or no, you don't know?"

"I don't know. I don't think so. I'm sure I would have heard."

"You say he said something about 'You know him.' Do you have any idea what he might have meant by that?" Stark asked.

"All I know is is that we had never heard the Mage like that. He was always—he was an inspiration to us all. He had such control of his life, of—of life." She raised her hands as if in invocation.

"So, whom do you think killed him?" Stark said.

She turned and looked dismally at Stark, shaking her head slowly. "I don't know."

"Could it have been someone in the group?"

"No," she said quickly and adamantly.

"Couldn't have been someone who wanted to be the Great One? Isn't there something about killing someone to steal his power?"

"That's just outsider talk," she snapped. "Persecution."

"Did he have any enemies in other groups, any rivals

178

in the movement?"

"It's not like that in our way of life. We have no envy. We are one with the universe."

"It does look like a ritual murder," Pearce said.

"That's ridiculous," Pender said.

"So, why are you so frightened?" Bradley asked.

She didn't answer.

Stark said, "Do you think you might be in danger?"

After a moment, she said quietly, "I don't know."

"Look," Pearce said, "Ms. Pender, if you do know something, or suspect someone, the best way to be safe is to tell us, because the only way you're going to be safe is if we lock the person up."

"I don't know anything more than I have told you."

****

The employees in the circulation department of the North York Advance weren't quite as helpful as Ted Henry had told Stark they would be. It turned out the errant bundle of newspapers that contained the serious error had been dropped off somewhere between Don Mills Road on the east and Yonge Street on the west, and between Sheppard Avenue on the north and Lawrence Avenue on the south.

"Great," Stark said when the circulation manager described the extensive area.

****

It took Harris most of the day to trace the phone numbers that George Sloane had listed in his little book. The Ottawa numbers had been assigned to various government offices over the years. He eliminated most of them—ones like the Parliament Hill buildings and grounds department. When he got to one with the Department of Industry, Trade and Commerce; one with the Department of Agriculture and one with the Department of National Defence, he thought he might have what he was looking for. When officials of all three told him he would have to go through their legal departments to obtain a list of everyone to whom the numbers had been assigned, he called a cop he knew on the Ottawa force. In five minutes, the cop called Harris back with names, departments and numbers that fit the right time period.

"How'd you do that so fast?"

"Federal government phone books. We've got 'em filed from the beginning of time."

Chapter Fourteen

"So, what do we know?" Stark sat in his car in the parking lot at Ashbridge's Bay, talking to himself. He had pulled in there off the Lakeshore when an irate driver had honked at him, several times. Stark had realized he had slowed to a crawl while trying to put things together in his mind.

"We have these men, all violently dispatched from life, all connected in one way or another. Three of them had keys to a locker that once belonged to the late George Sloane, the father of one of the three, who also died violently in a hit-and-run, the perpetrator of which was never apprehended. We discover that Sloane the elder was an agent of espionage for the Soviets, a deeply planted agent with entrée to the halls of power. The three who had the keys had been employees of the federal government. George had their phone numbers in his little coded book. What's that mean? He was a spy, and they were spies, too? What else? They all went to the same upper-class school at the same time. Young Alan must have been George's pride and joy, a chip off the old block. Sloane and son, Russian spooks. Instead of coaching him at hockey, Sloane senior coached him at espionage. And he probably trained him in the communist art of polemics, trained him well enough that Sloane the younger persuaded his school chums to express their natural rebellion against parental ethics by becoming spies. They were selected for their abilities, and indoctrinated as freedom fighters for the workers of the world.

"So where does Mr. Evil fit in: Blaide, the kiddie-cuddling Mage?

"Well, he was at Cranmer, too, and we know he lured at least one young weakling into his grasp whose father would have been a terrific blackmail target for the Soviets. And we know that young Sloane was at one time a member of his little gay circle. And he very much had young Peter Livingstone in his clutches. Poor Peter kills himself and the father resigns his government post. I don't think any of that is coincidence, and I think Blaide's murder, despite its ritual appearance, stabbed in the heart with his own wavy knife, was to silence him because he panicked. If he didn't know the involvement of two of the victims, and chances are he didn't—he probably did know about Alan Sloane's connection to the chums in Moscow. The Madeleine woman, the member of the coven, or whatever it is, heard the Mage in a phone conversation that sounded very much like somebody who thought the walls were falling in on him. So, if he was talking to our killer, then he was signing his own death warrant.

"But what about the other former student, the younger one, Bruce Anderton? Where's he fit in? He's a wildcard, that guy. Maybe he was a latter-day spy. I don't know. And then there are the newspaper clippings that were used in the Sweet Thursday note. Not much help, but it's likely they tell us that whoever put the note together lives somewhere in an area of North York. So, where are we? Where the hell are we? We? Where the hell am I? Nowhere."

Stark got out of the car. He leaned against the fender. He was wearing only a brown corduroy jacket and black flannel pants. It was mild for December, but damp-cold there by the lake. Stark hated the cold almost as much as he hated the heat, but at that moment, he didn't feel it. Folding his arms against the icy breeze off the lake was an unconscious act.

"What a fool I am," he said aloud. "I have to do everything myself. I treat poor Noel like a gofer, leave poor Ted Henry dangling in the wind. The poor bastard has to deal with Peters. And here I am with nothing. Aw shit, who knows? Dammit." He slammed his fist against the hood.

A woman pushing a stroller looked over and began walking faster.

Stark's cell phone rang.

"You're not going to believe this one." It was Harris.

"What?"

"The real old Toronto phone number, Gladstone 2473? The Bell has all the old phone books on file, including reverse books. Guess who it belonged to?"

"I don't know. Who?" Stark said with exasperation.

"One Horace Anderton, address the Bridle Path."

"Jesus Christ, the butler, Unger. Calvin Unger." Stark's legs went wobbly. His head was moving from side to side, his eyes darting, images flashing in his mind. "Dammit. Now I remember where I saw that bastard. I knew the second I saw him at the house that I'd seen him before, but then he reminded me that I'd been there, to the house, on that jewel robbery thing last year. But, for God's sake, I saw him a hell of a lot more recently than that. Why didn't I—I saw the bugger at the curling club, Noel. He was at the goddamned curling club. Jesus

Christ. Let's go. Call for back-up. Tell them to meet us—where? Okay, in the parking lot at Edwards Gardens. That's just around the corner from the house. I want to be the first one in."

****

Four uniform cars and a detective car from 33 Division were in the Edwards Gardens lot when Stark and Harris arrived. An Ident unit was on the way. Stark told two of the uniforms to tape the Range Rover at the house.

"Keep out of sight. Follow my car and stop when you see me wave. There's no reason to believe he won't open the door and let me in peacefully. But as soon as I get in there, I'm going to cuff him, and I'll radio you to move in. All right, we're off."

Stark rang the doorbell. As he waited, something on the pavement in front of the door caught his eye—a cigarette butt. It didn't fit with the meticulous surroundings, not a Bridle Path sort of thing. Stark picked it up with his fingertips, studied it for a moment, and then stared into space, thinking. He gave his head a little shake, took a poly evidence bag out of his pocket and slipped the butt into it.

Unger wasn't answering his ring. Stark pressed the button again and waited. After a time, he knocked. Still no response. He looked through the window in the door. There were lights on, and he could hear a radio voice reading the news. Maybe Unger was having a bath or a swim or practising his squash game. Stark turned the door handle. The door opened slightly, and Stark heard a scuffling sound behind it and felt a pressure against the door. He pushed it and the grey cat he had seen on his previous visit came around the edge of the door, mewing

184

loudly and rubbing hopefully against the detective's legs.

"Look out, puss, I'm going to step on you." Stark called out. "Hello in the house. Mr. Unger. Calvin Unger. Hello there. It's Harry Stark, Detective Stark. Can I speak to you? Hello." No response. Stark began to go from room to room. He found his way to the pool and the squash court. No Unger. He heard Harris's voice in the earpiece of his radio.

"Is everything all right?"

Stark whispered an answer. "There's no sign of him."

At the end of the hallway on the second floor, there was an alcove at one side Stark hadn't noticed the last time. It led to a flight of stairs up to a third floor. For the first time since he had entered the house, Stark unholstered his gun. On the second step, the odour hit him. It was a smell he had encountered many times in the past, and it was unmistakable. Stark pressed the button on his radio.

"Okay, everybody in, but orderly, quietly. No gung-ho. Come up to the second floor."

When the rest of them had joined him, Stark said, "Okay, boys and girls, cover your noses, take a deep breath. If you're prone to puking, stay down here. Something's dead up there. All right, let's go." Stark covered his nose with his tie and led the way up the stairs.

Calvin Unger's suite took up the entire attic. It included a sitting room, a bedroom and a four-piece bathroom. French doors opened to a spacious balcony with steps leading down to the back garden. Stark stopped at the top of the landing. "Okay. Everybody stop right there." Stark went to the French doors and opened them. There were two filing cabinets and a desk in the sitting room. All the drawers were open and empty. Calvin Unger lay on the bed, fully dressed, except his feet were bare. His wrists and ankles were wrapped in duct tape and taped to the brass rails at the head and foot of the bed. His eye sockets were dark holes, the lids and eyeballs gone. His mouth was ripped in a ragged oval, exposing his teeth, as if his lips had been curled back in a furious grimace. Most of the flesh on his ears was missing, and looked as if it had been torn off. There was a black halo-like stain on the pillows and bedsheets beneath his head. In the centre of his forehead, there was a bullet hole. The cat had followed Stark. It jumped up on the bed and rubbed its head against Unger's cheek. Stark grabbed the cat and gave it to one of the cops.

"Put this thing in your car, and don't lose it. It's evidence."

****

"He was tortured," said Blinky Berman, the coroner, a cadaverous-looking man in a baggy suit, wearing the thick glasses that had earned him the sobriquet. "On the bottom of his feet. See the marks? Somebody's held a cigarette lighter to them. Many times, it looks like. But it doesn't look like some sicko getting his thrills. This looks like an aggressive interrogation technique."

"No other marks?" Stark said incredulously. "What about the face?"

"Is there a cat?"

"Yeah, it's in a scout car."

"That's what I thought. The cat ate him."

"What?"

"I've seen it before. This guy's been dead about a week. The cat was starving, so finally it munched on all the fleshy parts, the ears, the eyes, the lips. There are lots of accounts of it in the literature.

"He was in very good condition. How old was he?" the pathologist asked Stark.

"Seventy-five. At least that's how old Calvin Unger was. Chances are this guy wasn't who he was supposed to be."

"Oh yeah? Seventy-five. My God. He looks like he could be, maybe, sixty-five, but, wow, seventy-five. He'd be in damned good shape for a twenty-five-year-old. The bullet killed him, by the way."

****

"You're back on the Scotch."

"I've got to get the stink out of my nostrils, Morty. You'd be drinking carbolic acid if you'd gone through what I went through today."

"What?"

"I don't want to talk about it."

"Are you still seeing that woman, the good-looking one?"

"Mmm. I'm meeting her here." He looked at his watch. "She should be here."

Morty looked over Stark's shoulder and smiled. Long, slender fingers curled over Stark's eyes.

Stark said, "Ulysses, cut it out. You'll make Morty jealous." Diane Shapton bit Stark on the ear. "Ouch. Jesus, don't do that. I don't think I ever want to be bitten on the ear again."

"You don't?" Shapton said with mild surprise.

"Not after what I saw today."

"He's had it rough," Morty said. "Must have actually done some police work."

"Yeah, most of the time, I sit in doughnut shops."

"Well, Sid Holtzman's anyway."

"Who's Sid Holtzman?" Shapton said.

"He owns a local deli. How've you been?"

"I've been fine. So what's all this about ears?"

"Nothing. Forget it. You want a drink?"

Later, in Stark's apartment, when Shapton tried to initiate lovemaking, Stark pulled away.

"What is it," she said. "Is something the matter?"

"It's this case, that's all."

"How's it going?"

"We're getting there."

"Closing in on the killer?"

"Yeah, I think it's just about all wrapped up."

"Oh, that's good. Can you tell me anything?"

"Diane, I think it's all rapidly coming to a close. I'll tell you what. As soon as I know, I'll call you. I'll tell you before I tell anybody else, even my superiors, how's that?"

"Great."

Chapter Fifteen

It took forty-eight hours to get the results.

As he'd promised, Stark called Diane Shapton. "Can you get out of work now? I can tell you everything if you come to my place."

"I'll be right over."

They sat in the kitchen. Stark made a pot of coffee. They both lit cigarettes.

"How long have you smoked those things?" Stark asked.

"Camels? Since I was a teenager. My uncle used to bring them back from the States. You couldn't get them here, except in the big tobacco stores downtown or some hotels, like the Royal York. I started smoking at my uncle's place. My parents didn't smoke. I'd steal a pack from his carton. I don't know whether he knew or not, but he never said anything. When the other girls were smoking Craven A, I'd pull these out in a display of worldly one-upmanship. The taste for them just stayed. For a long time now, though, I've cut right down to no more than ten a day, unless I'm drinking or tense."

Stark got up, poured the coffee and came back to the table.

"You know how they say, 'cigarettes will be the death of me.' Well, that's what's happened to you."

Shapton shook her head. "What?"

"I guess you must have been tense, or had a couple

of drinks before you went to visit Calvin Unger."

"Who?"

"Yeah, that's what I wonder, 'who'? I don't imagine his real name is Calvin. Probably Boris, or Ivan, or something."

"Harry. What are you talking about?"

"If you hadn't smoked those Camels, I'd have never made the connection. I feel really stupid. The Camels did you in, Diane. When I saw that plain-end cigarette butt, it suddenly all came together. My ego had switched off my bullshit alarm. But the unfiltered Camel turned it on again. I'd been wandering around in la-la land, thinking you'd been really smitten by me and not seeing what was the obvious connection in this: you. What an idiot!"

"Harry, you're not making any sense."

"Oh, I'm making sense all right. You had a cigarette in the car when you went to see Unger. You smoked it up to the door, and then you dropped it on the ground and stepped on it before you rang the bell. I had them get the DNA from it and compare it with butts you left in my ashtrays. Good thing I empty them only at Christmas. Not a good thing for you, though. By the way, we know Calvin Unger did the killings, at least two of them. But you know that, don't you? What we don't know is why. We're hoping you can help there, Diane. It would go a long way to mitigating your sentence. What do you say? There's just you and I here, Diane. I haven't arrested you yet. Whatever you say is between us."

Shapton shook her head slowly and smiled.

"You know, you're a fool, Harry. Such a soppy sap. I feel sorry for you. I really do." She drew her right hand from beneath the table. It was holding a semiautomatic pistol.

"Jesus."

"He won't help you, Harry. You should have brought the troops and arrested me properly. But thank you, Harry. You do honour your promises to ladies, don't you? Harry Stark, man of honour. Makes me feel I owe you something. By the way, don't try anything stupid. You're too—" She made a vague gesture toward him."—out of practice? I, on the other hand—well, I am a little rusty, but I was so well trained—" She finished the sentence with a little curl of her lip. "I want us to move. Let's go into the front room. Come on." She gestured with the gun, and Stark stood and led the way.

"Okay, pull the blinds closed and sit on the couch." She switched on the ceiling light and a pole lamp behind a wing-back chair, and sat in the chair. "The light's behind me. It's easy for me to get up, and difficult for you."

Shapton took a deep breath, held it, and then let it go in a long, loud sigh. "Harry, Harry, Harry—" She shook her head. "What am I going to do with you? You're terrible at taking directions, you know that?" She looked at her watch. "Well, I'm not on a tight schedule. The least I can do is put you out of your misery. Oh, I don't mean I'm going to shoot you. No, I mean the misery of not knowing what the hell all this is about." She took another deep breath, straightened herself in the chair, glanced at her gun as if making sure the safety wasn't on.

"All right," she said, "it all starts a long way back. I won't bother with years or dates. First, Calvin Unger. You're right. He wasn't Calvin Unger. I don't know what his real name was. He was a cut-off man. I saw in your notes the other night that you know that everybody was a spy, that you know about George Sloane. You sleep very heavily, Harry. Very useful. Your notes have helped me keep tabs on things. But your penmanship. Terrible. Thank you, Harry. Without your notes, I'd have never found Calvin Unger. I had no idea who he was. I knew he existed, but the only two people who knew his identity were his control in Moscow and George Sloane. But when Bruce Anderton was killed—I'm getting ahead of myself. Back to Unger. Unger gave Sloane his instructions, and he was the paymaster. They used Sloane's locker at the curling club as a drop. Unger put their pay in there, in cash, and they would collect it. Sloane, you know, was very deep cover. I'm not going to go into the stuff he was doing. I don't know all of it. My job was mainly recruiting. Two kinds of recruiting. I turned Chesley and Hawley, with help from Alan Sloane. His father raised him as a committed party man. I think he could sing The Internationale at the age of four: 'Arise ye workers from your slumbers, arise ye prisoners of want. For reason in revolt now thunders and at last ends the age of cant.' I won't sing it. I've got a lousy voice. "A school like Cranmer is a terrific source for revolutionaries and rebels of all kinds. You look for kids with a social conscience. They've witnessed the selfish arrogance of their parents. Most of them buy into the extravagance, but the odd one is disgusted by it. You seize on those ones.

"The other kind of recruiting I did was with people like Edward Blaide. He was a homosexual and a bit of a paedophile and, of course, there was the witchcraft crap." She shook her head. "He was perfect. We blackmailed him. I turned him in to the school authorities, knowing that they would push him out quietly, and then I saved his ass by providing him with a glowing recommendation for the public board. Alan Sloane being gay was a big plus for us. You know, I think his father even encouraged it because he could see how useful it could be. We got pictures of young Alan and Blaide together. Alan was a minor, of course. We had Blaide good. And then we looked for suitable candidates to send his way. Peter Livingstone was one such. He was a bit of a flop because he killed himself before we could get to his father. You know who his father was, of course?"

Stark nodded.

"Well, we had many others. Well, not many, but enough, that we sent to the Mage. We had a good thing going there for years. And then, it all ended. Glasnost, perestroika, the breakup of the Soviet Union, and it was over. A lot of people went back. But people like me, well, I was born here. I was turned in university. I was into all the Vietnam War protests, black power. I marched in Washington, got laid in a sleeping bag in front of the American consulate. I was a perfect candidate. The guy who turned me had a body like Adonis and was hung like a horse. The truth is, he was the one who got me hooked on Camels. He was an American. Well, he was Ukrainian really, but planted at an American university.

"Anyway, I had nowhere to go back to, so I just settled in to a bourgeois life and thought it was all over. And it was, until Unger began killing people. When you came to me and told me the names of the boys—I'm getting old—the men who had been killed, I knew, of course, what was happening. At least, I thought I knew what was happening. For some reason, somebody was systematically getting rid of everyone in our cadre.

Naturally, I thought my name would be on the list." Absently, she pulled a pack of cigarettes from her coat pocket and held them in her left hand and stood up. "I think well on my feet, Harry.

"Of course, I couldn't say, 'Oh, Mr. Detective, please protect me; I was a spy for many years, and I think I'm going to be killed, too.' So, I had to protect myself in two ways. First, I had to make sure you didn't find out about our little group; and second, I had to find out who was doing the killing and get rid of him before he got rid of me. Edward Blaide and his little scandal popped into my mind, and I sent you scurrying off in that direction. Those badly typed reports were my handiwork, ten minutes after you left my office. I thought the bad spelling was a nice touch."

She looked at her pack of Camels and back at Stark, raising her eyebrows.

"Calvin Unger. Well, Unger had a similar sort of problem to me. I thought it was the same problem, but it wasn't. Anyway, he had to conceal the real reason for the killings, so he thought he'd make it look like a serial killer was bumping off young, successful men. You know why he did it on Thursdays?"

Stark didn't answer. Shapton shrugged.

"I hope you're not sulking, Harry. You can't blame yourself; you were out of your depth. I'll tell you anyway. There was no clue in the text of the book Sweet Thursday. The title was symbolic. He thought it was ironic, or poetic or something. You see, old man Anderton gave him Thursdays off. So the worker used the day his capitalist master gave him off to kill symbols of capitalism or something. Not really, though, because the killings certainly weren't politically motivated, nor were they connected to his work as an agent. They were for a much different reason.

"Unger had a vault full of money. He was the paymaster, but all the money was laundered through George Sloane, through his various businesses. Over the years, Unger had skimmed off quite a nest egg for himself, and when everything ended, he decided to go into comfortable retirement. The only person who knew who he was in this country was George Sloane. Unger killed George and Annabelle. Arranged to meet them, and then ran them off the road up north. With George Sloane dead, there was no one to point a finger at Unger. Alan Sloane, Chesley, and Hawley didn't have a clue who he was, so for years, Unger didn't see any need to deal with them. It was all a bit ironic, because their killings had nothing whatsoever to do with their espionage or even their indirect link to Unger. It was Unger's greed that did them in. As time went by he began to be afraid that eventually they'd find him and make him share the loot. A great patriot of the people."

She paused to light a cigarette, held the pack out to Stark, who was sitting on the edge of the couch, his torso leaning forward, held stiffly, unnaturally.

"You want one?"

Stark shook his head quickly, almost a nervous twitch. His eyes were darting, not looking at Shapton.

"Bruce Anderton wasn't involved in any of this stuff. I made that up about his involvement in the occult, and the fact that he was a Cranmer alumnus was pure coincidence, but it did lead to Unger's plan. It seems that Horace Anderton trusted the old retainer implicitly, and he let Unger keep the household books. But Unger wasn't as loyal as the old man thought, and he didn't limit his skimming techniques to the operatives' payroll. Over the years, he bilked a small fortune out of the old fellow.

"Now, when Horace died, Bruce examined the old man's financial records. As you know, he was a forensic accountant, and it seems he spotted some irregularities. He was going to do a complete audit, which he foolishly mentioned to Unger, who suddenly pictured himself being unceremoniously removed from his luxurious sinecure and slammed into prison, and not even an Order of Lenin to show for all his years of devotion to the Motherland and the party. So he decided he had to get rid of Anderton. But he figured that if he just killed Anderton straight out, he'd be at the centre of the investigation, so he came up with this bizarre plan.

"He figured four birds with—I was going to say one stone, but he only used the stone once, didn't he? On poor Nigel Hawley's head. He was trying to make all the deaths look bizarre and sort of amateurish. He thought if he established the pattern and sent the silly notes that you'd think Anderton was just one of the string. In fact, he wasn't finished. I saved some poor sap's life by doing in Calvin. He had his eye on somebody else, completely unconnected to the others, but a young, successful businessman and an athlete. I don't know who it was. That would have taken you way off the path, and then he was going to pull in his horns and go to ground. I think he'd have pulled it off if he'd been able to cover all his old tracks, but, obviously, he didn't.

"You found George Sloane's notebook at Alan Sloane's sister's place. It was the one place Unger couldn't get into—all that security. He knew the book existed, and that he was in some way identified in it, and after he killed George Sloane, he looked for it, but couldn't find it. He said he worried about it at the time, but nothing happened, and the years went by. But then it began to weigh on his mind that one of the three, Sloane, Hawley, or Chesley, had the book, and maybe all three had been studying it to try to figure out who he was. He decided to remove the threat by killing them. Later, he got nervous that one of them might have had it in his house. So he broke into Alan Sloane's and then Hawley's. And he got into Chesley's by posing as a police officer. And your place, by the way. That cop you said the guy saw sneaking in your back door—that was Unger."

Stark shook his head.

"Oh, Unger was well trained. I imagine he got his training in the same place I did. They took me to the Soviet Union, you know. Six months in a camp northwest of Moscow. My God, it was rough. Sixteen hours a day. They beat you and then they loved you, and then they beat you. And they indoctrinated you. Showed you films of imperialist oppression, gave you history lessons. I came out a real hot-to-trot commie. I still am, actually, but you've got to live in the real world, don't you?" She stubbed out her cigarette and immediately lit another one. "You sure?" she said, holding the pack toward Stark once more, shrugging when he didn't respond.

"Where was I? Oh yes, Unger. Yes, I knew Unger would be very good at what he was trained to do, despite his advancing years. So, when you appeared and told me that three of my erstwhile agents had been done in, I got bloody scared. I knew that somehow 1 had to find whoever was doing the killings before he found me, and

I knew the only one it could be was the cut-off man. He was the only one of the crew, beside myself, still alive. It was Bruce Anderton's death that gave me the clue. You see, his death didn't make any sense. It didn't fit. He wasn't even remotely connected with our little organization. He was associated with the other three only in that he had been a student. I couldn't figure it out. And then—there it was, a gift from Harry, my knight in shining armour. I read your notes about interviewing the butler—the butler. That was it—it all came together. I remembered something that George Sloane had told me years ago. Because he thought it hilariously funny, and because he was quite pleased with himself, he told me that he had been able to get the cut-off man the perfect cover job: a butler. So, here's the anomalous Anderton—and he has this oddly behaving butler. Bingo. You know how I got him on the bed?" She smiled coyly.

"Jesus," Stark said with a look of disgust.

"He was a dirty old man, your Unger. But in great shape. If I'd had more time—anyway, I pretended to be both pissed and scared to death. He knew who I was, of course, and I told him that Sloane had given me his address. I told him that I knew he'd killed them and that I didn't want him to kill me. I told him I'd do anything he wanted, that I'd be his lover. It was all rather unbelievable, but I'm pretty good at that, don't you think?"

"You bitch," Stark said.

"Don't be bitter, Harry. You'll spoil the story. Anyway, I convinced him that I was a snivelling weakling, prepared to do anything to stay alive and started taking my clothes off. As soon as I got him on the bed, I shoved the pistol in his mouth. It's amazing how cooperative people become when they're gagging on a gun barrel. I taped his hands and ankles. Then he started to babble his story as fast as he could. He was doing the pleading now, saying that he had no intention of killing me, that the killings had nothing to do with the cell, that he had killed the three simply because he wanted to keep all the money and he'd begun to worry about the notebook and all the stuff I've told you. He said he knew all about them and where they lived, and their killings could be made to look like a pattern. I didn't believe him, of course—well, I did half believe him, but I had to be sure, so I did some nasty things to his feet with my lighter. It's incredible how the techniques come back so readily. He told me the whole story that I've told you.

"And then there was the money. He told me he'd stolen a lot of money. I knew he must have kept it in the house, in cash. I know the way these guys think. So I began to pretend to soften, began to let him think I was going to cut him loose and leave—no hard feelings, let bygones be bygones. We were even smiling at each other, and then I said, 'Wait a minute, the money. I want some of that money'."

"'Cut me loose, and I'll get it'," he said. 'Oh, sure,' I said, and back and forth, and then I threatened to burn his balls. I put the flame on his feet again. He gave in. I convinced him that I was prepared to release him. He told me where the safe was, told me the combination. I filled a garbage bag with it. Seven-hundred-and-twenty-three-thousand dollars, Harry.

"So that's the story, and everything would have worked out fine if I hadn't started smoking again. I've quit twice. Well, it looks as if I'm going to have to make myself scarce, doesn't it? Fortunately, I do have an escape package. I dug everything out the very day you came and told me about the killings, been carrying it around with me ever since. It's rather an old set of arrangements, but it will still work. I'll soon be a whole different person in a country far away. Well, goodbye, Harry." She raised the gun.

"Wait—" Stark held his hands up. "Blaide—you haven't told me about Blaide."

"Blaide? Oh, you mean the knife through his heart? That was me, Harry. Oh, sorry, that was I. Didn't you realize that? Yeah, that was all part of my misdirection effort. I knew I was going to have to kill him, make it look like suicide, make you think he was the one responsible for the killings—I tried to convince you that they were ritual killings, remember? And then he called me, scared to death. He'd read about Alan Sloane's murder, and he saw these cops following him. Your cops. And he said a new member had suddenly shown up, who had a rather weak provenance. That was Harris, of course. I wasn't really ready to do the deed, but I knew you were closing in on him, and that he'd crack wide open, so I arranged to meet him at his place, and gave him a ritual ending. Very convenient of him to be having a bath when I arrived a little before our scheduled appointment. So there you are, all wrapped up. You've solved another one, Harry. Listen, thanks for the fun. And it was fun. It really was. You're pretty good, you know. But you shouldn't drink beer before you go to bed. It makes you snore and fart in your sleep. Of course, you won't have to worry about that, will you? Goodbye again, Harry."

She held the gun at arm's length. There was a knock on the door.

"Jesus," Shapton said. "Don't fucking move a muscle, and keep quiet."

The knock came again.

"Harry, it's me." It was Noel Harris. "I know you're in there. I saw your car. Wake up."

Harris knocked again, louder. Shapton's head instinctively jerked slightly in the direction of the sound. Stark tried to roll to the floor. Shapton shot him in the head.

Chapter Sixteen

Detective Noel Harris pulled up the collar of the olive-green overcoat he'd bought himself to celebrate his making it up to full detective rank, and a member of the Good Suits to boot. Unlike Harry Stark, Harris planned to live up to the nickname. To that end, in addition to what he'd laid out for the new overcoat, he'd also paid a bundle for two suits, a taupe and a navy. It was a bitterly cold February, and the wind was looking for victims on College Street as Harris ran across it to headquarters. It had been six weeks now, but he still couldn't shake the image of Stark's blood-covered head.

On the day Stark was shot, by the time Harris had found the key Stark had given him and got the door open, Shapton had already gone through the back door. Hearing the shot, Harris's immediate thought had been that Stark shot himself. At first, he tried futilely to kick the door down, and finally dug in his pockets for the key. He burst into the apartment and rushed to his friend's side. He grabbed a pillow from the couch and pressed it against the wound, fishing out his cell phone with his other hand and calling for help, holding his ear against Stark's chest and hearing the heart still beating—weakly, irregularly, fading. Tears streaming down his face and praying out loud—more like pleading, begging—Harris didn't move from the spot until the paramedics arrived.

It took them a week to put some of it together. With

the help of Ernie Kowalski, and the grudging and limited assistance of CSIS, and the fact that Diane Shapton had disappeared, and the statement from Jimmy Yu, the dentist whose practice was downstairs from Stark's place, who said he had seen her arrive before Stark was shot. It turned out that the security service had a file on her, skimpy, just suspicions. There was no evidence of her having actually done anything, and because there was an unofficial grandfather agreement among Cold War antagonists, they had left her alone.

"Jeez, it's bitter out there," Harris said to Ted Henry.

"Mmm?" Henry looked up slowly from his newspaper. "Is that a new coat?"

"Not bad, eh?"

Henry pointed an avuncular finger at the young detective. "Don't go into debt. Some of these guys in here have got bigger wardrobes than Sean Penn." He paused. "They found her car in Fort Erie, by the way."

"Fort Erie?"

"It was parked at a twenty-four-hour Tim Hortons near the bridge. The place is so busy round the clock, they didn't notice it until this morning. Somebody looked inside, and that's when they called the cops. It seems that all her cards, her credit cards, driver's licence, library card, social insurance card, everything—they were all lined up on the passenger seat, in rows. What the hell do you think that was about?"

"I don't know. She could have killed herself, I suppose, and this was a way of symbolizing that her life was over, that these were the only visible milestones of her life."

"Why would she go to Fort Erie to kill herself, for God's sake? No, she was rubbing our faces in it. That's what she was doing." Henry leaned back in his chair. "I called CSIS this morning, and they think she would have had a whole set of identification as somebody else. It'll be Canadian, and she'll have kept it current, renewing the passport when it came due; same with a driver's licence. She wanted us to know that. Her little joke. She probably walked across the bridge, or more likely took a bus to Cleveland or somewhere. She's headed somewhere she can disappear, Costa Rica or— someplace like that. I think we've lost her."

"So, it's over," Harris said to Henry." Not a good way to end it, not at all. He must have wanted a better way to go out."

"Oh, we're not going to remember him for this. He never had a case he didn't solve. Not one. We'll remember him for that. Of course, most of them never liked the bugger. There's a lot around that'll be glad he's gone. He was always too smart for them, and he let them know it. Let me know it, too, but I never minded. As long as he solved the cases, that's all I cared about. He was good at it."

"What a sad way to end it."

"Anyway, we'll take care of everything. We'll give him a big send-off."

"I can hear you bastards," Stark said, his voice muffled by bandages and the whirr of hospital monitors.

"You're awake?" Harris said.

"Of course I'm awake. I'm waiting for that nurse to come in and check my catheter again. What's this 'big send-off' crap? I'm not going anywhere. You dicks can't get rid of me that easily. I'll be as good as new in a couple of weeks. I never used that part of my brain anyway. It's only for numbers, and I never could add. Now, get the hell out of here, and send that nurse in. Is somebody feeding my cat?"

"I leave her food, but I never see her," Harris said.

"Just make sure you feed her. I don't want the bloody thing to eat me."

* Ed. Note: Lester Lanin died in 2004 at the age of 97

A word about the author...

John Worsley Simpson was a journalist--reporter and editor—for many years with major-market newspapers in Canada and the U.K. and with Bloomberg News. He has several published novels, including Undercut, which was runner-up to Kathy Reichs' Deja Dead as best first novel for 1997 in the Crime Writers of Canada Arthur Ellis Awards. Other traditionally published novels include Counterpoint, Shadowmen and A Debt of Death. Another novel, Death Never Says Goodbye, was published through Amazon and Create Space. He is married and lives in Barrie, Ontario, Canada with his wife, Colleen, and dog Measha.

http://www.johnworsleysimpson.info

Thank you for purchasing
this publication of The Wild Rose Press, Inc.

For questions or more information
contact us at
info@thewildrosepress.com.

The Wild Rose Press, Inc.
www.thewildrosepress.com